Detour Trail

by

Joy V. Smith

Published by
Melange Books, LLC
White Bear Lake, MN 55110
www.melange-books.com

ISBN: 978-1-61235-570-2 Print

Published in the United States of America.

Cover Art by Becca Barnes

Detour Trail
Joy V. Smith

Westward bound on the Oregon Trail, Lorena Emerson is alone after her uncle is killed by a thief trying to steal his money belt. Ignoring the wagon master's advice to go home, she rounds up others needing help, and they join a later wagon train and are soon slogging through dust and mud and steep mountain passes. It's a long way to Oregon, and because another woman needs her help, Lorrie again goes her own way, leaving the wagon train and the Oregon Trail to travel onward—off the beaten path—with her small group of wagons. She's helped by members of her wagon train, people she meets along the way, and the mule, Jake, an integral part of the story. You'll meet them as they join in her travels and encounters with enemies and as she searches for a new home and supplies as winter reaches out its icy hands.... Settling the frontier isn't easy!

Chapter One
~ Starting Over ~

"I'm sorry, Miss Emerson, but with your uncle dead, you can't travel with the train any longer. You'd best sell your livestock and wagons and go home and find yourself a man to take care of you."

Lorrie Emerson attempted a smile. "Thank you for your concern, Captain Mead. I understand that you don't want me tagging along. Good luck on the rest of your trip."

The wagon master nodded and rode back to the wagon train, and Lorrie's smile died as she considered her options. Returning home was not one of them. With her uncle's help, she'd escaped from those other uncles and aunts who wanted to take her in and have custody of her and her inheritance. However, David Emerson was a lawyer and succeeded in extricating her from their attempts to corral her. They'd decided on heading west before that was a sure thing, and then they liked the idea so much, they sold everything they could and left Pennsylvania and headed for Independence, Missouri.

The Oregon Trail had been a magnet for settlers looking to obtain some of that fertile land in Oregon Country since the early 1840s. She hadn't expected her uncle to be so enthusiastic, but as he told her, with all those settlers and all that land, a lawyer would come in handy. Now he was dead because of a thief who'd seen his bulging money belt and snuck into his wagon and killed him in the ensuing struggle. Her uncle was a stubborn man; of course he fought back.

She'd been relying on him for a long time. And she might have saved his life if she hadn't hesitated. He'd taught her to use a gun, but she'd never killed anyone, and anyway, she hadn't recognized the danger in time, so it was a wagon train guard who'd killed the thief. She'd retrieved the money belt before her uncle's body was removed, and now it was fastened around her waist under her skirt; and God help the man who attempted to take it from her.

So, David Emerson was now buried back along the trail, and she hadn't taken the time to cry yet. At least, she thought, Mead hadn't dumped her until they got to this little settlement along the North Platte River. It'd probably blow away in the next strong wind. She looked at the two wagons, hers now, along with the four oxen that pulled the big wagon and the two horses that pulled the smaller wagon. She needed help. Was a man the answer? Then she spotted the two boys playing Kick the Can under the shade of some trees near the river.

She gave a piercing whistle, and when they looked in her direction, she waved them over. She'd been afraid to leave the wagons and livestock untended, which had kept her from exploring and learning more about the town. The bigger boy sauntered casually over, followed closely by his companion. She saw now how ragged and filthy their clothes were. Not hampered by anyone who cared, she decided.

"Can you help me?" she asked the older boy.

"What do you want?" he asked warily as his companion squatted next to him and drew circles in the dirt.

"I thought you would know what happens around here. My name is Lorrie Emerson. Will you tell me yours?"

"I'm Timmy; he's Jason, and we know a lot. You're going back east. Do you want to sell your stock? Do you want us to find you a buyer?"

"What makes you think I'm going back?" she demanded. "Maybe you don't know as much as I thought." She half turned away.

"What we don't know, we can find out," Jason said, standing up, and she realized Timmy wasn't the only one making assumptions.

"Okay, you know I'm alone—and now you know that I'm not going back. Are there others stuck here like me?"

"Yeah, the two negroes—slaves maybe, that ran away. Their wagon broke down and they got left," Timmy added.

Jason nodded. "And the brother and sister, but they lost their horses and wagon 'cause Colly took them."

"Why couldn't they take them back? Can't someone help them?"

Lorrie wondered if this little town was even more backward than it looked.

"Colly's got two men almost as mean as him; the marshal's out of town, and Colly scared the brother by threatening the sister. They're both scared of Colly for some reason. I don't know why they didn't sneak up on 'em and shoot 'em." Jason would have done that, she surmised, and Timmy would have backed him.

"So, can you tell the negroes to come see me and the other two? Do you know their names?"

"The negroes are called Brown; I heard someone say that; then they laughed. And the brother and sister are the Michaels. He's Dennis. We'll find out the rest of their names. Are you paying us for working for you?" he asked casually.

"Of course. We'll see what you can do, and we'll decide what it's worth." Lorrie thought they could be worth it, and she saw that they were eager to have something to do besides earning cash money. She'd have to have their money out for them before long. She'd learned to be careful about that.

Before supper time, which for her meant stale bread and cheese and water to drink, Timmy was back with a black man. He eyed her camp thoughtfully, before coming up to her. "The boy said you wanted to talk to my wife and me," he said politely. 'Course you understand that she had to stay with the wagon and horses."

"I understand; that's why I asked you to come see me. I didn't want to leave my stock. I'm alone. They said that you got left behind too. I'm Lorena Emerson, by the way."

"Evan Brown," he told her, and looked at her wagons hungrily. "They tell you our wagon broke an axle and smashed both rear wheels? There's a blacksmith in town, but we don't have enough money to fix the wagon and buy more supplies. We've been living on what we had since we got left."

Lorrie was debating whether to leave Evan Brown at her camp while she went to see theirs when Jason arrived with a red-headed pair who must be the Michaels. She was slender and tall, and he was at least half a foot taller. They both looked undernourished. Colly must have taken just about all they had.

Lorrie moved forward to welcome them. "I understand that you've lost all your supplies," she said. "I think maybe we can help each other. I have two wagons and need drivers and some help."

Evan Brown lost no time in joining them. "My wife and I can drive, and she's a very good cook."

Lorrie laughed. "Oh, now you're in for sure, but I'm not thinking just about two wagons. Why don't we all camp together and start working together. I don't suppose, Mr. Brown, you can haul your wagon over here, so maybe we should join you there. How's your campsite? Near water? Clean enough?"

The black man looked relieved. "We're upstream from the town so we're clean enough, and we can move the stock. We can go now, if you like."

Lorrie nodded slowly. "Wait here a minute, if you all would. I have to talk with my crew." She glanced at Timmy and Jason, who'd been watching suspiciously, probably wondering if they were no longer of any use, and if they were going to see any money.

Lorrie led them out of earshot and sat down on the ground. "You've done well," she told them, "and I deeply appreciate it." She'd seated herself with her back to her flock, and now she handed a dollar to each of the boys and set her purse on the ground between them. "I'm going to give you some more money now for the future. It's called a retainer. Now I want you to keep an eye out for chickens, food supplies, wagons, and whatever you think I might be interested in. But the most important job—and this might be too hard for you—is to find me a man—a trustworthy man—who can help me get the Michaels' belongings back. Probably we'll need more than one." She watched and waited to see how they would respond.

They'd been hanging on her every word, and now they sat back a little and looked at each other. "You picked the right men for this job," Jason said. Timmy didn't nod as he usually did, but his eyes glowed with enthusiasm. "And we can find the man you need. Just one, I reckon."

"I'll be at the new campsite. We'll talk privately so as not to worry the others."

"Of course," Timmy breathed, and Jason nodded. She had given them not only money, but value and a purpose. She was a little worried about the fire she'd lit.

Later, when her little party had driven the wagons to the campsite, she studied the Brown's wagon and frowned. Hannah, who'd been waiting and cooking a stew that smelled so good that everyone's stomach snapped to attention, stiffened. “T’ain’t much, but Evan built it with his own hands out of wood we found.”

Lorrie turned instantly, “Of course, I can see that. I mean it’s a good wagon. What I was wondering was—is it worth fixing?”

“We gotta fix it. No choice.” And Hannah stood straight and proud.

“Uh, Mrs. Brown, I’m seeing choices here. I’m looking for maybe one or two more wagons—one would be yours—and all I want for that is to eat at your campfire. Naturally I’ll furnish the food. But look at the wagon. How about if we took it apart and carried the wood and good axle as cargo—for building and maybe repairs.”

The couple looked stunned. He moved first, putting a big brown hand tenderly on the tilting wagon. “I’m Evan, Miss Lorrie, and she’s Hannah, and I think that’s a good plan. Where you gettin’ the wagons?”

“I’m scouting for them and maybe more livestock. We’ll see what we need. I heard there’s a small train a few days out. I’d like to be ready to join it.”

“No sense wastin’ time,” he agreed with a smile. “So we might as well get started on supper.”

After wiping out her bowl of stew with her stale bread, which she’d contributed to the common larder, along with dishes for the entire party, it was time to go to bed and be rested for whatever might happen on the morrow.

Lorrie was up early to be ready for the boys, but when they didn’t show up, she did her wash at the river and spread it on nearby bushes to dry. The deliberate crackling of brush prepared her for their arrival, but when she turned around her smile vanished as she eyed the wiry man in buckskin who smiled down at her. “Morning, ma’am,” he said.

She inclined her head. “I’m Lorena Emerson. Are you looking for me?”

“Yep. The boys said you needed me.” When he saw her wariness at the mention of the boys, he added, “Timmy and Jason sent me. I’m Bolt.”

“Any significance in the name?” she asked.

“Some, but that’d be bragging.” Lorrie blinked, then went to untie Shadow from the wagon tongue. As she saddled her, Bolt brought up his horse, a big bay that nuzzled the mare until Bolt mounted and pulled him away.

“Did they tell you what I need?” Lorie queried. “There are at least three men—mean ones, Timmy said."

He shrugged. "I looked in your wagons and saw two rifles and some guns. You any good with them?"

"My uncle taught me along the trail."

"Want to show me how good you are?"

"No, I don't waste bullets."

"You don't have enough to waste?"

"Who does," she said offhandedly, beginning to enjoy the game.

"Want to get it over with?"

"Might as well. I don't have a lot of time. Do you have a plan?"

"Well," he said thoughtfully, "you could back me up." Thinking of what might lie ahead and hoping she could rely on him and also herself, she hesitated and he raised his eyebrows.

"I'm thinking," she told him with lifted chin, "that I could go in first and brace them, get the lay of the land, maybe get them off guard, and even get the drop on them, and you back me up after scouting their camp and seeing how much of a threat there is. Oh, you haven't asked about payment."

"Naturally that'd depend on if you even needed my help," he said. She just knew he was laughing inside.

"The thing is, if they see you that could affect the outcome, I'm guessing, without you actually doing anything. We have to consider that."

"We will," he promised her. "So what are we planning to take away from them?"

"Carrol would have come to show us, but her brother wouldn't let her. Apparently Colly made some nasty remarks, and Dennis wants to keep her safe."

"Not a gentleman then," Bolt said, and his demeanor hardened.

Lorrie suddenly felt more confident, but she merely said, "Their team is a pair of black Shires. Big, they said; their names are Abe and Sarah. Carrol's horse, Firefly, is a sorrel with a white star on her face. Pewter is a gray gelding. I'd be tempted to take any that look like that and sort them out later."

"Good plan. Timmy checked on their camp this morning; they were all there then. Jason is keeping watch. Timmy went back to join him. And we're almost there. Going in on horseback is best. How's your horse around gunfire?"

"No problem there." Lorrie didn't say that most of her practicing had been on horseback. "But we'll have to take time to hitch the team to their wagon. Drat. That makes it iffier."

"No problem. They'll do the hitching."

"Oh. Good plan. Um, so you're not planning to kill them?"

"If need be. You object?" His tone sounded as if he would think less of her if she did.

"Nope. I'd feel safer if I didn't have to worry about them coming after us, but that's no excuse to kill them." She hoped she didn't sound as if she'd be disappointed. She didn't want to feel responsible for a massacre, but she would like to know what he planned.

"We'll see." He halted his horse shortly behind a clump of trees and brush and pointed to where three men lounged next to a small fire, drinking coffee and frying bacon. She'd remember that smell connected with the scene for a long time, she thought. And then Bolt slapped Shadow on her flank and Lorrie moved into the clearing. She didn't stop until she was close to the fire. She reined the black mare in, grateful that the men were all on the same side of the fire, 'cause they'd been dishing out beans and bacon. Now the biggest man, who had a scar on his left cheek and was shirtless, put the coffee pot back on the fire. No one spoke; they were puzzled, not suspicious.

She turned Shadow and brought up the gun she'd been holding next to her leg. She had a rifle in the saddle holster, but you don't use that for close work, her uncle had told her. (He'd defended a few criminals in his day.) "I've come for my nephew's horses and wagon," she told them, and she smiled with her mouth, but not her eyes. "Get them now."

All three men moved. The little one spoke, "They were a gift from a lady friend," he said, and leered at her. Oh, that was Colly.

"Don't tempt me, Colly," she said. Her voice was ice cold—from excitement and anger. "I want an excuse to shoot you. Whether I kill you or not, I haven't decided yet. Now stop wasting my time."

The three men all laughed at the same time and began separating. She'd noticed at the start that they were all armed, with a rifle leaning against a wagon just behind them, though they ignored it. I'm taking that wagon, she thought, and felt herself getting more excited than was smart. She couldn't wait, and she remembered what had happened the last time she'd hesitated, and so she shot Colly in the leg.

That wiped the smiles off their faces, she thought with satisfaction, but then all three drew on her. Who to shoot next?! Her gun wavered, even as she knew she was too slow. Shots rang out from beside her then, as Bolt raced his horse up next to hers. Two more men were wounded, before they listened to Bolt's demand to drop their guns. Colly was last to act, and so she shot him again, aiming for his gun and hitting his hand. The gun fell from his hand—or what was left of it.

All three men stared at her in horror, and she wouldn't have been surprised if a similar expression was on Bolt's face. He was shaking his head as he dismounted. "I would have warned you," he told the men, "if I'd thought you'd listen." We didn't plan to hurt anyone. All you had to do was harness the horses and let us take her nephew's belongings back to them. Now I have to do it," he said in annoyance and he kicked one of the men as he walked by him. "Better bind up his hand," he told the other one.

Behind them, before he harnessed the horses, he turned and winked at her. She smiled in response, and the men on the ground shuddered. Before long the wagon was loaded with everything the men eagerly pointed out, and the saddle horses tied behind the wagon, and Bolt drove the wagon away, leaving Lorrie to cover him. The three men left behind didn't so much as quiver as she backed Shadow away. She was glad to see that Colly's hand was wrapped. 'Course she was also glad that he wouldn't be able to use it for a long time, if ever, but she told herself that she'd have to exercise more control in such situations.

Bolt drove the wagon back to Lorrie's camp, and she trotted alongside until he pulled up near the rest of the livestock. Neither spoke until he dropped off the wagon seat and walked back to his horse. "That was sure something else, Big Boy," he said to the horse. He looked up at her and shook his head. "I sure wondered if you were going to kill them all," he remarked.

"No, it wasn't my plan. I hoped I wouldn't have to because I didn't want to leave bodies lying there, raising questions."

"And drawing flies. I'd have charged you a lot more if I had to clean up."

She nodded. She felt better now that the excitement and anticipation had drained away. "How much do I owe you," she asked him. "After all, you did have to harness the horses too."

He shoved his hat back and looked thoughtfully at the ground. "I think twenty dollars should cover it."

"You're sure? I couldn't have done it without you. I was worried that they'd come after us. I'm not so worried about that now. What do you think? And what about that lawman that's supposed to be around here? Is he liable to cause you any trouble? I'll probably be down the trail before he comes back. What about you?"

He smiled at her. She thought he'd just barely been able to stifle a laugh. He slid his hand into his shirt pocket and pulled out a piece of metal. After he polished it on his sleeve, he showed her the shiny badge. "I think you can stop worrying about that," he told her with a grin.

She looked at him in chagrin, before relaxing into a grin herself. "Well, I'm relieved about that. But do lawmen get paid? I mean, you've earned it. I just wondered, but I'll get it now."

He stopped her with a touch on her arm. "I would have done it just for the fun of it," he said seriously, "but out here we don't always get paid, and I can use the money for ammunition and food for Big Boy. Also, if you didn't have the money, I wouldn't have asked—or not for as much."

He knows I have money, she thought, because of how freely she'd talked about buying more wagons and supplies to the boys. Be more careful, she chided herself.

She started for her wagon again, but stopped, being reminded of the boys. "What about Timmy and Jason," she asked him. "Is anyone caring for them? I wondered about that the first time I saw them."

Bolt shook his head. "Their mother was, ah, a saloon girl; she died last year. Kicked to death by a drunk. Their father was long gone, whoever he was."

"What happened to the drunk?"

"Sad to say, he died before he got to the jailhouse. Kicked by a horse, the doc said." And he scratched Big Boy's head.

"How sad," she said, looking away from his horse's big hooves.

Bolt shrugged. "About the boys. I'm glad you asked, and I saw how they've been working to help you. I think I'll deputize them. Better to have them working for me than running loose and getting into trouble."

Lorrie looked at him and decided to give him the forty she'd thought about earlier. She climbed into the big wagon when she reached it, and pulled the canvas shut behind her. She rattled the strongbox bolted to the wagon bed. It held some money, but was mostly a distraction. She counted out the forty and wrapped it in her biggest handkerchief.

He was waiting beside Big Boy, who was drinking from a bucket of water that apparently Timmy or Jason had brought, as they were waiting there, too. She handed him the package, and he hefted it, then looked at her with the rise of his expressive eyebrows. "It's for you and Big Boy;" and she nodded casually at the two boys before giving him a meaningful look. "I owe you both a lot," she told the pair, "and I will never forget how you made it possible for me to get back on the trail." She handed each boy a handful of silver coins.

"Thank you, Miss Lorrie," Timmy said dolefully. Jason just hunched his shoulders and turned away.

"Bolt told me how you helped him too, when we had to go in to retrieve Dennis and Carrol's horses and wagon. I told him that you were the most helpful and smart men I'd met on the whole trail so far, and he said that he'd noticed that. I think he's hoping that you would help him now."

Both boys turned in a flash and looked at Bolt with anticipation. "Yep. That's what I said, and I hope it's not too soon for you to start. Big Boy here, would be happy to have fresh straw in his stable when we get home later. I have to buy some supplies now." He swung up onto the saddle, and as an afterthought, added, "I've got an extra room for you, if you want. It'd be more convenient for us if you were nearby when I needed you. Save me a lot of time tracking you down." And before he rode off, he winked at Lorrie.

Chapter Two
~ Back on the Trail ~

Timmy and Jason found time to continue helping Lorrie and her group to buy two more wagons, chickens for Hannah, and other supplies. The Browns' team was hitched to one of the new wagons, and the disassembled wagon and good axle were loaded into it. Bolt brought her two horses for the other wagon and said only that their former owner didn't need them anymore. Lorrie laughed at him, and he smiled back, saying, "Now don't you shoot anyone 'til you're well out of town."

Getting ready for the new wagon train, loading and distributing supplies and furniture and working with the new team, Cherry Pie and Dandy, found them almost ready when the train arrived. This wagon master, Colonel Dawson, was eager to have them join his train. "Two wagons broke down and had to be left along with their contents; three families turned back at the last settlement, and there's a pregnant woman who's wanted to stop for miles now." He shook his head. "They were all ill-prepared. I should never have taken them on, but it was getting late. The smart ones leave in spring."

Lorrie nodded. "I know." That's what she and her uncle had done. It took at least four months to get to Oregon Country, and now it was almost the middle of June, and it was miles to South Pass.

"Let me take a look at your group. I don't need to be slowed any more." He was impressed by the livestock and wagons, however. He glanced at the brother and sister. "They look young to be on their own. And what about them?" He looked curiously at the negro couple.

"The youngsters are my niece and nephew, and I'm responsible for the others too."

"Good. I'll just worry about the rest of my flock then. We leave in two days—at dawn. I wouldn't wait that long, but we need supplies, and the livestock could use the rest and time to graze."

The grass was wet with dew as they harnessed the horses and oxen. Evan helped with the oxen after he'd hitched up his own team. "Strong looking, all of them. What are their names? I'll need to know if I'm to drive them."

"The two red and white ones are Jemmy and Dolly; Jemmy has more red. Clay is the brown one, and Spotty is the black and white. They were named when we bought them," she added. "Hannah won't have any trouble with your team?"

"Never. Peter and Paul—she named 'em—are as gentle as you could wish. And we'd been taking turns."

"I see. I'd switch off if we could, but with all of us driving, that's not possible. I want to be sure we've got enough wagons if one breaks down," she explained. "Also, my uncle had heard that settlers had to dump a lot of furniture when that happened so we started out light. We didn't have much to pack anyway. And he thought we might pick up any good stuff we came upon. No need for it all to rot, he thought."

"Your uncle was a thoughtful man, I reckon."

She looked at Evan. "You have no idea. I miss him a lot, but I'm more than grateful for the people who've helped me since then." Then it was time to line their wagons up, but Lorrie took a few minutes to jump off her wagon seat when Timmy and Jason came up. They were carrying a box with holes.

"It's for you," Timmy said. "It's two hens ready to lay, and you can cook 'em if you have to. We heard they'd come in handy."

It's a gift," Jason added, so she'd know not to offer them money.

"You couldn't have given me a better gift," she exclaimed. "My uncle and I did start out with a little flock, but we let them out one evening to feed and never saw them again. Never heard a sound either."

"Not smart," Timmy told her. "Be careful with these uns."

Jason nodded. "The marshal gave us money," he added. "We didn't steal em." That sounded like they had in the past, but didn't want her gift to be tainted—or to have Bolt down on them. She smiled and exclaimed over the chickens again, but didn't hug the boys. They probably expected to be treated as men.

"Good-bye to you both, and be sure to say good-bye to the marshal for me."

"He had to go after some bandits down river," Jason told her in explanation.

She would have told them to take care of him, but that might cause them to go help him, so she didn't. They'd gone after him before, she knew.

After that they started, not dawdling because by then the Colonel was there frowning at them. Evan went first with the oxen, followed by Hannah driving Peter and Paul, Lorrie driving Shadow and Sunny, Carrol driving Abe and Sarah, and Dennis driving Cherry Pie and Dandy. They weren't the last wagon though. That belonged to the Johnson family, which included Samuel Johnson, a very pregnant Elizabeth Johnson, and their three boys and a daughter.

"Mrs. Johnson says she's suffering enough. She don't need dust in her face too," the Colonel told Lorrie, explaining the lineup and why the Johnson's wagon hung back, before galloping to the front of the train to get it moving.

Sunny, Lorrie's red roan, was frisky when they started out, but she settled down after a few miles, and the Colonel, who'd been keeping an eye on the newcomers, finally left Lorrie and her team to check on the others.

It didn't take long for everyone to get into the routine of hitching up, pausing for a break on occasion, and then unhitching and rubbing down the animals before going to the campfire where Hannah was cooking supper. They all took turns caring for her team so she could concentrate on feeding them. She tended to see that they were all tucked in too, though mostly they were grateful to be lying down rather than being tossed to and fro as the wagons went up over bumps and down into ruts.

The days were always the same except when it rained, and the wagons bogged down in the mud. Fortunately the trail paralleled the river so far, and there was plenty of water for washing and for watering the animals and keeping the water barrels full. The days were punctuated now and then by the moans and cries of Mrs. Johnson.

"How far along is she, Hannah?" Lorrie asked after the woman had come back from taking food to the Johnson wagon one night.

"Too far to go back, and forward's a long ways too." Hannah looked back worriedly at the wagon. "Bout eight months, we figger."

"Didn't she know she was pregnant when they started?"

"She wasn't so far along then, and they got a late start 'cause one of the kids was sick. The youngest boy, George. Now she wants to stop. She says the land looks good enough to her. They can't stop by their selves though."

Oregon Country's looking farther away than ever, Lorrie thought, and they were still on the plains, though there looked to be mountains in the distance. Some sort of rock formations anyway.

A couple days later the mountains loomed closer. She was wondering about them when Colonel Dawson halted his gray horse next to her wagon and hauled himself onto the wagon seat next to her. "We're coming up on Mitchell Pass," he told her. "That's pretty steep. How are your people holding up?"

"We're fine, and the horses and oxen are in good shape too. They're thinner than when we started, but they don't run away when we bring out the harnesses."

"Too tired, I expect. You're all doing well. I just wanted to check on how you were feeling. Not everyone is doing as well," and he looked back.

"We've given her some mattresses," Lorrie said. "I think that's helping." Mattresses were just some of the things she'd picked up along the way. The other members of her party had started doing that too.

"Ah, she has sounded quieter. Thanks." And he made an agile leap onto the gray that had been keeping pace with the wagon.

It wasn't long before they could see the rock formation. Chimney Rock, the wagon master told them. And then they began the descent. That's when they almost lost Elizabeth Johnson. The mattresses began sliding toward the front of the wagon, and her children holding on tight, was all that kept them in the wagon until it leveled off.

"She's not looking too good," Hannah told Lorrie that night. "And the Colonel is beside himself, not knowing what to do."

Lorrie shivered. "Is she likely to lose the baby?"

"I hope to God not," Hannah said, with a desolation in her voice that startled Lorrie.

"Have you ever had children, Hannah?"

Yes. They're long gone."

"I'm sorry. Did they die before you decided to go west? Is that why…"

Hannah looked at her. "They didn't die," she said flatly; "they was sold," and Lorrie saw hot anger in gentle Hannah's eyes. She flinched.

"Not your fault, child. Nothing to do with you." She touched Lorrie's arm to reassure her before turning away to look again at the wagon. "What can we do?" she asked despairingly.

Lorrie wondered, too, and remembered other hard choices she'd made. She decided to talk to Elizabeth Johnson. Later that evening, when Samuel Johnson helped his wife carefully out of the wagon to relieve herself as far away from the wagon as she could walk, though it looked rather like an uncomfortable waddle to Lorrie, she approached the couple. "Why don't you see to the children, Mr. Johnson, and I'll stay with your wife for a while."

Elizabeth Johnson looked at Lorrie, who'd loitered discreetly nearby, after pulling herself to her feet, which were shod only in slippers. "I'd be happier not go back in that horrible box," she said bitterly.

"But can you hold on a little longer," Lorrie asked, "if you knew that we could stop sooner? And not go through another upsy daisy pass?"

"Where?!"

"I don't know yet. It's too soon, you know that. This is not a good place, and I can't wait to get away from it. But further along towards the mountains, or at least the foothills. We need time to look around. I can't promise anything, but there are settlements and forts here and there farther along."

"He wants to make a good home for us. In a place that's good for the children—all of them. He's worried sick for me and the baby, and he's so sorry that he brought us along, but I was the one who wouldn't stay behind. I wanted us together. It probably doesn't look that way to you, but it's not his fault."

"I see," she said. "I did wonder. Okay. We'll just sit here quietly and think about the future—and the baby's future. And I'll ask the colonel about Indians."

Lorrie continued thinking after Mr. Johnson had come to fetch his wife. She thought as she studied the landscape, thought about her little flock, and pestered Colonel Dawson with questions. They were still headed north along the Platte towards the mountains and surrounded by territories that would someday be states. Before long they'd drop south and continue their journey westward.

"A respite before we tackle South Pass? That's still pretty far, and I don't want to waste time."

"Resting the animals and letting them graze while there's still plenty of grass isn't wasting time, sir. And though Mrs. Johnson seems better, her whole family would appreciate the rest too."

Colonel Dawson considered her thoughtfully. "I don't usually let people tell me how to run my train," he told her. She blinked and wondered how else to approach the subject.

"But I see that you're thinking—maybe planning—something, and since it is a good idea, we'll stop at the first good place with water and spend two days there—no more. There are some repairs to be made, and I'd thought about stopping soon myself," he added.

Men were interesting and sometimes fun, she thought to herself, and wandered back to her wagon. Later, after supper, she said casually, "The Colonel plans to stop soon for two days rest and repairs. I'm planning to look around then, maybe up in those foothills. There are lots of trees up there, but I wonder what else is here."

"Indians maybe," Dennis said.

"No trace so far, Colonel Dawson said. The scouts have been looking for sign."

Chapter Three
~ Scouting New Trails ~

The night they made their rest stop, after a supper of Hannah's savory stew and biscuits, Lorrie casually asked, "Does anyone want to look around while we're here? Those forested foothills to the southwest look inviting. I wonder if anyone has homesteaded around here."

"Are you thinking of the Johnsons?" Hannah asked. Lorrie wasn't surprised that she'd picked up her train of thought.

"We don't have to go to Oregon. After all, there are settlements along the trail."

"The land in Oregon territory sounds rich," Evan said bluntly. "We've seen lots of rocks along the way and there are mountains just ahead of us."

"I know," Lorrie agreed. "I thought we could look, though."

"We can tend the camp and do those repairs on the wagons, and I've got mending and cleaning to do. Let the youngsters have some fun and look around, Evan."

He sighed. "Must be nice to run off and play,' he said grumpily, "but take care of your horses. Shadow's got to be able to pull the wagon after you've run her up and down those hills, Lorrie. At least Abe and Sarah can take it easy while you're gone."

"Thanks for looking after them. We wouldn't go if we couldn't trust them to your care," Dennis said.

Lorrie tied Sunny up before she left; the other horses and oxen weren't interested; they hardly looked up from their grazing. "Splitting up would let us cover more territory," Lorrie said before they mounted their horses, "but it might not be safe."

"Carrol stays with me," Dennis told her. "You, I won't worry about so much. Hills aren't so good for farming, and there's a whole lot of trees to clear up there. I thought we'd follow the river a bit and then check out some of the creeks. We'll need water. We're camping out tonight so that saves us time."

"We'll meet back at camp then. We need trees for building cabins, good level land for farming, and water. I'll look for deer trails."

Lorrie zig-zagged Shadow along the hillside she'd chosen to explore. Going straight up would be hard on her horse and wasn't likely to lead anywhere useful. I don't see how we can find anything even if it's here, she thought. What was I thinking?

Late that morning she let Shadow choose her path. She'd be more likely to find water at least. When the mare stopped to sniff the air, Lorrie loosened the reins. Water must be nearby, she thought, but the horse looked up the hill and whickered.

Lorrie had a gun in her belt; it was hidden by her jacket. It was a good thing she hadn't taken it off yet, even though it was getting warmer.

"Stop fooling around, girl," she said sharply and headed the horse downhill. She'd make better time when the land leveled out. However, a black and white horse emerged from the trees just ahead of her. The rider wore buckskins and his long brown hair was tied back. He was fast and intent on stopping her, she saw, so she pulled Shadow up and held her at an angle.

The rider held his hands high and to the side though, guiding his sure-footed mount with his knees. "I'm sorry if I scared you," he said gruffly. His beard wasn't as long as his hair, but it was thinking about it. "I'm figgering you're lost or looking for something."

Lorrie smiled innocently, keeping her hand on the pistol. "You live hereabouts?" she asked brightly. "Are there other homesteaders here?"

"Not so many. Mostly it's me and my family. I've been watching the wagon train, and I saw you three heading away. What'cha looking for?"

"The land is pretty, but awfully hilly. Any valleys around? How's the water?"

"There are two big valleys not so far from here. One has a fair-sized creek running down the middle to the river, and it carries down water from the spring melt so it floods. The other is broader; the river runs by at one end; the other end climbs gradually up. Enough room for a few farms, even a town."

Lorrie blinked. She was surprised and suspicious. "You make it sound inviting. I'm guessing you're a mountain man?"

"I hunt and trap, yes."

"Then why would you want to be crowded? I thought you mostly avoided civ… I mean crowds."

He nodded. "Mostly that's true, and my wife and I are happy here without the benefits of civilization," and his mouth quirked slightly, "but our daughter is growing, and I don't want her to be limited by what we're content with."

"I see." Lorrie wasn't sure she did though. "What's your daughter's name? And does her mother want her to be given these benefits?"

The mountain man stretched, leaning back in the saddle, and looked away for a couple minutes. "Want to see the valley? It's a ways, and we can talk as we go. I don't think you've got much time to waste."

"What makes you say that?" she asked, curious.

"I watch, I listen, I learn. I've seen many trains go by, but yours stopped here. That's never happened before, so I decided to find out your plans. The train is going on to Oregon, but you're exploring here. What does that mean?"

"Didn't you find out?"

"The wagon master's guards are good. As I crawled around in the dark, I caught only snatches of people's plans—and hopes."

"A few of us are thinking of staying—if the land is good. We are worried about Indians."

He studied the ground a few minutes. He's trying to make up his mind too, she thought. "No Indian problem here," he said finally. "They've mostly moved on." They rode on, and in a couple hours, she was pretty sure, he led her up to a rise where they could look over a valley that was green with scattered trees, though it was mostly grass and wildflowers. He pointed to the other side of the valley. "That used to be all trees too, but there was a forest fire almost two years ago. Easy to clear now."

"It's beautiful, but how's the soil? I don't want to lead my people to a wasteland." She didn't catch his sharp glance when she mentioned 'her people.'

"My wife has a garden; I hunt and fish; we eat well. If you're serious about being neighbors, we should introduce ourselves. If not, we can go our separate ways." He waited a minute, then turned his horse back up the slope.

"Wait! I was thinking too. How can one be sure of the path to follow?"

He looked at her and shrugged impatiently. "I found my path. I can't help you find yours."

"You already have!" she exclaimed, tightening her grip on the reins. "My name is Lorena Emerson. And even if we don't become neighbors, we could introduce ourselves."

"True enough. I'm Brock Summers. My wife's name is Many Stars; our daughter is Starlight."

"Beautiful names," she said softly. "And I would like to be neighbors, though I have to discuss it with the others. Can you tell me about water, game, Indians, the weather."

"My home is near a spring. There is another spring near what would be a good home site, and I think you would not have to dig deep for wells. Game is plentiful, though I travel far to avoid killing it off. My wife is Arapaho, and we have no quarrel with the Arapaho and have not been bothered by the other tribes. The weather is cold in winter. You'll need to build well and have firewood and piles of blankets."

"The sooner we start, the better then, to prepare for the winter. Can you help us with the planning and maybe the building? I would pay you, meaning no offense, but the laborer is worthy of his hire. I don't want you thinking we'd take advantage of your generosity."

"You speak for your people then?"

She realized that she was planning for them, and said ruefully, "I can't, and they will want to meet you. Will you come with me to our campsite?"

He shook his head. "I will need to talk with my people too. Like you, I have planned for them." He knew Many Stars would be afraid, but Star was lonely and restless, though she would be reluctant to leave her mother.

Lorrie didn't waste time retracing her trail after Summers pointed her in the right direction. She'd have plenty of time to think and worry on the way back, and she wouldn't spend time looking for the Michaels siblings. They might have an interesting report also. Is there enough time to build and plant before winter? No one could predict Indians. She tried to remember what the colonel had said about the tribes in the territory. She did remember the Arapaho tribe, now that the mountain man had mentioned the name.

She slowed Shadow to a walk as she approached the wagons. She didn't see Firefly or Pewter, Dennis' gray. Well, naturally not. They'd be camping out. She hadn't seen any point in her doing that after meeting Brock Summers, and this gave her a chance to talk to Evan and Hannah first and get their opinions. She'd already decided that she wouldn't try to persuade anyone one way or another. She didn't want the responsibility.

"What do you think?" Hannah asked her after she'd reported on her scouting trip.

Lorrie leaned back. "I don't know. What do you think?"

Evan looked up from his plate of chicken and biscuits. Lorrie was glad she'd made it back in time for supper, and that they'd decided to kill another chicken, though this meant that they'd have to find more. "You were there. What did you think of the man? The valley?"

"The valley is beautiful and broad, and there's a river. I'd like to look at the other valley, too, even though he said it floods. It might be useful for grazing in summer or for farming. He seems trustworthy and intelligent, and I feel that he cares for his family, but worries about how they will be treated. He was weighing the consequences of encouraging me to stay."

"We need to stay close," Hannah said, "and visit his family. We'll learn more then, and making friends with them would be wise. What do you think, Evan"

"I like the idea," he said slowly. "Here we won't be competing with other farmers. We'll have first choice. I like that, I admit. We hardly had any choices before now."

Hannah looked at him and nodded. "If they're worried about what we think of them, it's not likely that we need worry about what they think of us. And I think we're far enough from back there…"

"I want to do it," Lorrie told them a little later, after giving them time to think, "but I don't want to sway anyone. What about the Johnsons? Should I talk to Elizabeth now or wait for Dennis and Carrol?"

"We'll wait," Hannah said decisively. "Let them think about the future without us shoving a choice in their faces so soon."

"I feel like waiting," Lorrie told her, "also like having more of that chicken and biscuits."

"We need more chickens and pigs and cows. We're short of livestock for farming."

"We'll cut our cows and pigs out of the train herd," Lorrie said in surprise.

Evan looked at her and smiled. "We need breeding stock," he told her.

"I should have bought more," she said in dismay. "The cows and pigs are mostly yours. I was focusing on supplies and scavenging." She'd had a good time picking up a couple dressers, a box of dishes, four beds, and several chairs, plus the mattresses. It was Evan who had made room in the various wagons for three cast iron stoves.

Chapter Four
~ Laying Foundations ~

Dennis and Carrol got back late the next day. “Lots of trees for building, but they’d be green, and we didn’t see much level land,” Dennis reported.

“My fault,” Carrol said, “I wanted to go higher up and find a lookout, but the trees and the rocks kept getting higher too.”

Lorrie laughed. “We’re getting close to the mountains, but I found a valley that might do.”

Carrol looked at her and smiled. “So you went down.”

Lorrie shook her head. “Nope, you give me too much credit. I found a guide. Well, actually, he found me. He’s been watching the wagons and us and thinks we might make good neighbors.”

“He wants the whole train?” Carrol twisted the end of her pony tail. “They’re not going to stop. It’d just be us and the Johnsons.”

Lorrie sighed. “I haven’t even talked to them yet. I’ve been waiting to hear what you thought. And there’s not enough time for you to look at the valley, and I’m not even sure I could find it again!”

“Did he say anything about a trail?” Dennis asked.

Evan stood up and looked at the Johnsons’ wagon. “I reckon he’ll find us and show us a trail, but you need to talk to the Johnsons first, anyways. I still see a lamp lit over there.”

Lorrie looked at Hannah. “Will you walk over with me?” she asked hopefully. Hannah nodded, and they walked towards the wagon with children spilling in and out of it.

“The kids have lots of energy. They’ll help too. It’s not all on your shoulders, Lorrie."

"Thanks, Hannah. I'm afraid of making a mistake—a horrible mistake. You know—I think shooting people is easier than this."

Hannah looked sideways at her. "It's true then? That's how you got their wagon and horses back?"

"I had help!"

"And you've got help now. You just tell them what you found out, and I'll be here to hold your hand if you need me."

"I think it's a good idea, when I'm not afraid." Then Rollie, the Johnson's oldest boy, saw them and called to his parents. Samuel Johnson poked his head out of the canvas at the rear of the wagon.

"She's feeling poorly," he said softly, "but I think she'll be glad to see you both." He climbed down and gave the two women a hand up.

Inside, Elizabeth Johnson was lying on the mattress pile. She turned over and said fretfully, "It's time to go outside, Samuel, and maybe I'll just sleep under the wagon so I don't have to get up any more. I have to go out too often, now." She tried to sit up then and saw them.

"I found a valley today," Lorrie said. No point wasting time. Mrs. Johnson needed encouragement at least. "It's empty, with hardly any neighbors. We'd have to do all the clearing and building ourselves, and it'll doubtless be hard to get the wagons there, but it's closer than Oregon. But I'm afraid there's not enough of us to start a settlement."

Mrs. Johnson sat up, and Sallie Sue, her oldest girl, clambered up the mattress pile to hold her up. The girl looked hopefully at Lorrie. "When can we start?"

"Tomorrow morning," her mother said firmly. "The Colonel stopped by this afternoon to check on me. He didn't shake his head in despair, but I think he turned away so quick so we wouldn't see him cry. Tell him tonight, Lorrie, so he can get a good night's sleep before starting again in the morning."

Lorrie swallowed. "Okay, I surely will. It's nice of you to think of that, Mrs. Johnson." She swung down out of the wagon and looked at Hannah, who'd followed her down. She felt a little panicky, but Hannah grabbed her hand and held it while they walked up the line to Dawson's wagon.

The colonel was staring glumly into the fire and sipping a cup of steaming coffee. He stood up when the two women approached; he did not look hopeful. "Evening, ladies," he said.

When Lorrie hesitated, Hannah stepped forward. "Glad tidings, Colonel. The Johnsons and all of us will be pulling out in the morning too, but taking a different trail."

The colonel was obviously torn between relief and worry. "You think that's wise?" He frowned and stared at the ground. "You know I'm relieved not to have the responsibility for getting her through South Pass or even any further down the trail," he confessed. "I'll not try to dissuade you. I just hope you know what you're doing—and where you're going!"

"We have a plan," Lorrie said reassuringly. Or it would have sounded so if her voice hadn't wavered a bit.

"Not to fret," Hannah said, and they didn't know which one she was addressing. Possibly both. "We should all get a good night's rest so we can get an early start in the morning."

"Bless you, Mrs. Brown," the wagon master said when they turned away to go back to their wagons.

"Thank you, Hannah. I'm tired enough to go straight to sleep, I think." When she crawled into her blankets though, Lorrie was sure she wouldn't sleep, but next thing she knew, she smelled sausage simmering in Hannah's skillet.

Sausage, eggs, and fresh corn bread got Lorrie's mind off what to do next. She took her time over breakfast, and what she noticed first after that, was three cows and two pigs tethered to the Brown's wagon tongue. They were the Brown's, and the wagon train was mostly a cloud of dust in the distance. She started up in dismay, and then she saw her cow tied to the small wagon's tongue, while the Michaels' two cows were tied to the back of their wagon and their little piglet snuffled noisily in the dirt near the two sows.

"Evan got all our livestock at first light," Hannah said, as she finished shaking out their bedclothes and piling them on the wagon seat. She stopped and looked at Lorrie. "He's wondering when we're going to start. He doesn't want to hitch up the horses and oxen too early."

Evan appeared behind her carrying two water buckets. He poured them into the water barrel, and turned to Lorrie. "I've topped them off and taken the animals to drink. What direction are we headed?" He waited to give her time to think of a response.

"We'll backtrack my trail and get started now. Sooner started, sooner finished. And, Evan, you're wagon master. We won't waste any time if we have someone in charge who knows what he's doing."

Both the Browns stared at her in surprise. Then Hannah said, "That's a good idea. I'll finish packing."

Lorrie was relieved to have someone else in charge. All she had to do was to pick a direction. She was pretty sure that Brock Summers would appear along the way; he might want to be sure of them before he showed up.

But before they'd finished hitching the teams, Clifford, the Johnson's middle boy, called out, "Rider coming." Lorrie looked up and recognized the black and white horse loping toward them. The rider pulled up beside the closest wagon, and the Johnson children started climbing out until their father called them back.

Lorrie walked immediately over to Summers. "I'm happy to see you," she said And very relieved, she thought to herself. She turned to the others. This is Brock Summers, our guide." She introduced him to the others—"Evan Brown, our wagon master, his wife, Hannah, Dennis and Carrol Michaels, and the Johnson clan, starting with Samuel and Elizabeth Johnson. You can sort the kids out later, along our trail."

He nodded. "Pleasure to meet all of you. It'll take most of the day because I've picked out the easiest way. I chopped down a few trees to make it quicker."

Before the day's end, the wagons were in the valley bottom, not too far from the river to make watering the livestock easier. Elizabeth Johnson had her husband take the canvas off their wagon to make a tent. "Now that I don't have to climb in and out of that wagon, I won't!"

Chapter Five
~ Building Begins ~

After setting up their camps, they gathered at the Brown's for supper. The setting sun bathed the valley walls in a golden light. "Tomorrow we make plans," Lorrie said. She'd been thinking about their settlement for some time. Well, it wouldn't be a settlement for some time, but they'd make a start.

After breakfast would be the time to discuss what they wanted and needed to do, Lorrie announced. It certainly wouldn't be before they ate. Afterwards, they settled down in front of the Johnson's tent. Since Elizabeth didn't feel up to walking far; she sat in the doorway. "First of all, does anyone have any ideas about where and how we should start?" Lorrie said. "It's getting late in the season, though it's sooner than it would have been in Oregon territory. We need to plant and build."

"You're right," Brock Summers said. They hadn't seen or heard him arrive, but now they saw his horse grazing with the rest of the livestock close to the river. "It gets cold here. You'll need plenty of firewood and snug, tight houses and barns to keep your animals warm and safe. Feed for all of them will be a problem. You'll have to make what hay you can. The planting comes first. You can't tell when winter will come. Sometimes it's early and sometimes it's late, but you have to be ready."

"Can you show us those home sites you mentioned?" Lorrie asked him. We'll need to clear land for houses, crops, and pasture."

"Use the valley for pasture as long as you can," he advised. "And fence some grass off for hay. And don't forget, you don't have stores here, blacksmiths, or doctors. You have to do it all yourself."

"We're going to build down here in the valley," Elizabeth Johnson announced. "And what you said about stores, Mr. Summers, sets my mind on what Mr. Johnson and I were discussing last night. We'll build a store; it'll be a house and store. Two stories; we'll live on the bottom 'til the top is on, and then the store will be on the bottom, and we'll live on top. And then someday, I'll have a brick house further up the valley."

Good plan, thought Lorrie. We need a store. "Have you thought about stocking it, Elizabeth?" she asked. "You know I have extra furniture, dishes, linens, etc. We can trade, if you want."

"Thank you, Lorrie. I had thought of that," she admitted. "We'll have food from our garden; the kids can take care of that. The youngest are too young for building and plowing anyway."

"Lizzie will be good in the store," her husband added. "We decided that we'd rather do that than farm, and a store is a good thing to build a town around. But what gets built first?"

"I was thinking, even before I heard your idea, that your family should have one of the first houses. I will have to be last because there's only one of me, and I'll stay with someone until my house is built."

"You can stay with us," Carrol said. "We'll sleep together, and Dennis will have the loft."

"Thanks, Carrol."

Evan Brown stood up. "You said, Lorrie that Mr. Summer spoke of a spring. I'm asking that Hannah and I have that site. It's time she was able to take it a little easier. We'll wait for our house if we can have the spring."

"That's a good plan," Lorrie said enthusiastically, "especially since a cook needs to have plenty of water. I only ask that you have us over to supper now and then."

"Any time, child. I don't like to think about you trying to cook!"

"Well, you have taught me all I know about cooking, but it's too early to send me off into the world on my own." Everyone laughed, and little George rolled on the ground and giggled. All knew that she didn't want to cook. She'd pull one of the wagons herself before she'd cook. They knew that because she said so.

* * * *

The planting came first, and then they cut trees to clear the land around where the cabins would stand. There'd have to be room for gardens and barns and corrals. They pastured the cows and horses in the valley as Summers had suggested, using logs for fences. The oxen also dragged logs wherever else they were needed.

They knew they'd need cellars for storing food and keeping the cabins warm, but digging takes time so they started the Michaels' cabin on ground level; it would be a barn later. The Brown's cabin would have a lean-to for the animals with a barn also built later. Lorrie contented herself with choosing a home site on a small rise with a creek running at the bottom of it. "It'll have a porch running the whole front," she told Carrol when they'd taken time off to visit it.

"Are you going to save some of the wood from the wagons for that?"

Lorrie looked at her friend with worried eyes. "Using that wood for floors is helping us with building 'cause the logs are so green, but we have to save at least two wagons for hauling. And we're going to have to haul in supplies and get more cows and pigs."

They both knew that they were using up their foodstuffs faster than they could grow them or butcher. "Hannah doesn't want to kill any more of her chickens, and we'd be in worse shape if Mr. Summers didn't drop off venison now and then," Carrol said.

"I've been thinking about that," Lorrie told her. "We can't spare any of the men. Evan's either making shingles or helping lift the oldest logs so we've got walls on three cabins."

"Two cabins and a barn," Carrol reminded her. "Oh, I'm not complaining, but when winter comes, it's going to be awfully cozy with the three of us, two cows, and little Piggy, who's growing all the time."

"We'll use the wagon boards for a loft to sleep in, but I'm hoping we'll have time to finish the Brown's cabin and the Johnsons' house and start on your cabin before winter. However, that's not why I made you walk up the hill to my home site."

"I did wonder, but I know how I'm looking forward to a real house of my own." Carrol put her hand over her mouth. "You know you're welcome at ours 'til you have yours."

Lorrie nodded, and thought that her plan would give the siblings a respite from such close quarters in their barn home for a while, at least. "The leaves are beginning to turn, and Summers said again, that there's no way to predict when winter will set in. Sometimes it comes late and sometimes it just visits. In any case, we need more of everything, including nails. And so I'm taking my small wagon to do more scavenging back at the last settlement."

"Lotawater Creek?"

"Yeah, if I can't find much there, I'll have to go all the way back to Wayside."

"That's a far ways, and I never want to see that place again!" Carrol said sharply."

"No good memories there for you and Dennis," Lorrie admitted, "but I've got friends there at least."

"But who will go with you?!"

"I can't take any of the men away from the building. Even the Johnson kids are busy with taking care of Elizabeth's big garden. And Hannah has to stay, to be here for when the baby decides to arrive."

"It's gotta be any day," Carrol said, remembering how the pregnant woman needed help to go down the front stairs of her new home.

Lorrie nodded. "So I'm going to ask Starlight and her father if she can go with me. He did want her to see more of the world."

"You'll have to give her some of your dresses then."

"I packed several riding skirts, but maybe a couple dresses for town would be good. And maybe buy some fabric too. And see what her mother would like. Because she sure wants to keep her daughter safe." She smiled. "Her parents have taught her to take care of herself. Have you ever seen how she uses her belt knife? I've asked her to teach me."

"The men won't like it," Carrol warned her.

"Which is why I'm not telling them. I'll take a load of shingles down to the Johnson's and keep on going. I haven't told Hannah because she'd tell Evan. Once I'm gone, they'll be less apt to worry."

"Probably, but I'll make up for them. Be careful!"

"You can bet on that, and now I'm riding up to see the Summers. You can go back to your cabin now and work on fences for the corral."

Carrol wrinkled her nose. Rearranging fencing while trying to keep the animals from heading for the woods was no fun, but they weren't going to let them in the "barn" until they had to. "Thanks for the rest," she called out, as Lorrie mounted Shadow and headed up, "but not for the worry."

Lorrie slowed Shadow to a walk as she neared the Summers' cabin tucked among the trees. There was a garden down slope in a clearing, but the cabin was sheltered by evergreens. Smoke spiraled from the chimney so Many Stars was probably baking or cooking. Convincing her would be the hard part, and she couldn't even be sure that Starlight's father would allow it.

"Ho, Lorrie," came Star's cheerful voice as she rounded the cabin carrying a pan full of dripping meat. Lorrie glanced at the carcass remnants with distaste. She wasn't fond of cooking, but she'd sure never butcher. Star laughed at her expression. She knew Lorrie enjoyed eating at their cabin, but would do anything rather than prepare the food. "Father and I are butchering out back. He'll be up as soon as he hangs the rest of the meat up in the smokehouse. Mother's cooking this for lunch."

"I'm glad I'm in time for that." She blushed a little, chagrined that she was so lacking in the basics that Star could do so easily. "Maybe after you take that in, we can talk. I want to talk to you first."

Star was immediately interested, so it wasn't long before she came back out. "I have to wash up first," she said. Lorrie followed her to the wash basin on the back porch and rehearsed her speech while waiting. When Star looked at her expectantly, Lorrie walked back out front and fussed a little bit with Shadow's bridle.

When she finally got up the courage to turn around and face Star, she found her perched on one of the rocky outcrops that surrounded the cabin. "I need to go for supplies," she said without preamble. Star knew they were short. "I'm taking the small wagon because I have to leave the oxen for hauling logs, but I'd rather not go alone. I can use the company and help."

"You don't want to take any of the men 'cause they're busy. I usually help Mother get ready for winter too, but there's not so much left, and it can wait. You're not going to ask Father to go?"

"I know he's busy hunting—and helping us—a lot. He probably won't want you to go, which is fine with me. I just thought I'd ask."

"Wait here. I'll go help him in the smokehouse; I can talk to him there."

Rather than go in the cabin and face Many Stars, Lorrie unsaddled Shadow and groomed her while waiting. There was something soothing about combing a horse and not thinking about the future.

Shadow turned her head and looked at the cabin, and Lorrie saw Star and her father standing on the front porch. Brock Summers studied her soberly, and Lorrie thought about saddling Shadow and going home—or at least away.

Summers saw her nervousness and beckoned her over. “We’ll talk to her mother,” was all he said.

Inside the cabin, Many Stars was taking a pan of bread off the coals to the side of the fireplace, while the venison sizzled on the spit over the fire. Summers glanced at his wife and said, “We’ll eat first.”

After a meal that Lorrie appreciated despite her apprehension, Brock said, “Speak to your mother of your wishes.”

Lorrie figured he didn’t want to be the one to broach the subject. Star went to her mother and sat at her feet, speaking to her in what was obviously her mother’s language. Lorrie had never heard it before. It was a good idea, she decided, since it would save embarrassing their guest.

Finally Many Stars looked straight at Lorrie. “You will guard my daughter?” she asked.

“Of course! I wouldn’t take her if I didn’t think I could take care of her. Of course, I want her to guard me, too,” she said honestly.

“I would never clip my little bird’s wings,” her mother said, and that was settled.

“When do you leave?” Brock asked.

“Tomorrow morning. I know we don’t have time to waste.”

He nodded. He’d warned them often enough. “And where do you go?”

“I thought I’d go back to Lotawater, and if necessary back to Wayside.”

“They would build in the flood plain,” he mused and shook his head. “No, there are farms and small settlements near Fort Laramie. They supply the fort and the wagon trains. It is farther, but your choices are better. There may even be some hay there. I’ve talked to the trappers that get their supplies there. It’ll be rough getting to the trail, but once you‘re on it, you’ll make better time.”

Lorrie nodded in agreement. “Yes, thank you, and the wagon will be light going.”

The next morning, Lorrie drove the wagon to where Evan had a growing stack of shingles. The men loaded the wagon and sent her down the well-worn trail to what would be their settlement. Star joined her farther along. Her horse, Swift, was a pinto similar to her father’s. She was leading a pack horse. “Father said we should take Lightning in case we need him. He said that Brimstone could pack more meat if he killed some.”

"I'll thank him when we get back. I wanted to take another wagon, but we've taken apart most of them for building, and they can use the oxen and big wagon here for hauling."

"The little wagon will go better on the trails," Star reassured her. Before noon, they'd dropped the shingles at the Johnson's; the oldest children helped unload, and they were on their way.

They ate lunch near the river so they could water the horses; then they headed west to Fort Laramie. The journey was quiet and occasionally rough, but the days were still warm when they reached the trading post. They decided to ask to stay at the first farm they came across. The horses and wagon should be safe there while they rode Swift and Shadow to scout out the area. The Hansons were happy to let them stay after Lorrie arranged to rent the corral and pay for hay and oats and meals at the farmhouse.

"I think they might sell us that old cow. Even if she's not a good milker anymore, we can use her for beef," Lorrie speculated.

"And they have lots of chickens," Star said, "and did you see the geese? But what are those little chickens good for?"

"They're bantams. They must be good for something, and they'll be easy to carry. I've got a shopping list from Hannah for supplies, and we'll ask around and take whatever they have to spare!"

Chapter Six
~ Supply Run ~

Lorrie was glad to see that the store had plenty of supplies. "Most of the trains have gone now, and we've been stocking up for the next ones," the sutler explained. "Look around; I'll be out back if you need me."

"We should have brought the wagon," Lorrie said, looking around at the full shelves. There was sugar, salt, rice, tobacco, and more.

"We'll bring it tomorrow before more customers come, but we can load some sacks on the horses now."

"How can we scout for livestock while buying supplies, and how can we guard them?" Then Lorrie remembered how she'd used locals before, and she went outside. There were Indians, trappers, and probably some local folk. How to find them. There were only adults here to buy supplies too. She and Star decided to buy what they could and head back to the farm.

The wagon sat under a shade tree, with Sunny and Lightning in the corral. They unloaded the horses and turned them into the corral, too, before going up to the house to see if it was time for supper. It was, and the table was full of chicken, mashed potatoes, baked beans, gravy, hot rolls, and Lorrie smelled what she was sure was apple pie. She smiled happily at Star. And then a flood of children swarmed in.

By the time Lorrie had decided that she'd better join the crowd, the table was full of eager appetites. Mrs. Hanson bustled in with another plate of chicken and shoved it among the other brimming dishes. "Now we all sit down," and she gestured at two empty chairs at the far end. "You girls sit yourselves down too and join us in grace." She looked around to be sure everyone's hands were in their laps and not sneaking a forkful of food before squeezing herself onto a stool between two of the youngest. "For family, for friends, for food, and, of course, for the strangers among us, we thank thee, Father."

Even when she'd finished, everyone sat still and waited. Lorrie heard a man singing in the back of the house, and Mr. Hanson joined them. "You're late," but Mrs. Hanson said it gently, and Mr. Hanson held up his clean hands for her inspection.

"One must be clean, and I got dirty in the new field. Fencing is not an easy task."

"Did you finish, Father?" asked one of the older boys. "I can help you tomorrow."

He looked at his wife. "Have they finished harvesting the potatoes?"

"Oh, yes, and they weeded and started picking the beans," she said proudly. "Elmer and Norman can help with the fence tomorrow, if you need them. We'll start shelling the beans tomorrow night."

Mr. Hanson smiled. "I'd hoped to finish today, but that fence wire was just as determined not to let me. Having the boys hold it will be appreciated." He looked now at his guests. "Harvesting comes first; the winters are long and hard. Soon she will start the canning, one of her favorite chores." Everyone joined in the laughter, so Lorrie knew it was a family joke.

After supper everyone went off to do the evening chores, and Lorrie and Star asked if they could help. Immediately Star was helping the oldest girl do the dishes, and Lorrie went out with little Billy to put the chickens up for the night. She couldn't have asked for a better opportunity.

"Are you always busy with chores?" she asked the boy as she held the gate to the coop, and he led the chickens in with a scattering of feed.

"Most always, but we're not as busy in winter and we play games and sing and Mother reads to us."

"The thing is, Star and I need help with our chores, which is finding supplies for our settlement. Do you think your mother would let us hire you to help?"

Billy contemplated her with sudden hope. "Real money in coins, not paper?"

"Yes. It's not hard work like in the garden or making fence, but riding around to the outlying farms and seeing if they have what we need, and then bringing it to our wagon here. They'd have to bring the animals and food unless you could use your wagon. I wanted to ask you first because you know or could ask your siblings what they know."

"Where would I find a sibling?"

"I'm sorry. I should have said. A sibling is your brother or sister. It's quicker than saying your brothers and sisters."

Billy rolled the word around on his tongue with a new found happiness. "Sibling. So I have lots of siblings."

"I think so. Are they all here?'

"Not all. Some are working at the fort or guarding one of the wagon trains."

"I see. That is a lot of siblings."

"I can ride to the fort by myself," he told her. "And Melanie visits her friend at the Jensens sometimes. We can help. Let's ask Mother right now if we can do it."

When they went into the house, Mrs. Hanson was singing a song in a language Lorrie didn't recognize while she mended socks. Trousers and shirts were waiting for her attention. "The chickens are snug?" she asked.

"Yes, Mama, and Lorrie wants to hire us siblings to help her with her chores."

Mrs. Hanson turned a sock inside out and looked at the neatly mended toe while she considered what her offspring had said. "What kind of chores? They are young; I will not let them work hard after their own chores are done."

"I must apologize. I meant only for them to do errands for us because we have so little time to get everything done and then get back home before winter. I do need their help—or someone's help."

"Why can't I help, Mama?" Billy asked plaintively. "And Melanie. We can use the horses that aren't working."

"We will ask your papa. I think he will agree with me that our children can help others. It is a good thing to learn."

"I apologize again, Mrs. Hanson, but I wish to pay them for their work. I'm sure they have learned to be generous from their parents."

"You are paying us for your keep," Mrs. Hanson said firmly. "I do not know why you speak of our generosity."

"You and your family have made us feel welcome. You can't buy that, and we both know that you need money to meet the needs of a large family, though you work hard to take care of them." Lorrie didn't mention the sons working and probably supporting their family. She'd only now thought about why they weren't working on the farm.

"My children do like earning money and helping out, and you need to get back home. Winters are hard here. Will this be your first winter out west?"

"Yes. I have been warned, but the weather has been warm, and the leaves haven't started turning yet. Well, I saw a few."

"It likes to sneak up on you, so Billy, tell your father what the ladies want, so he can make his mind up on the way back from the barn. Off with you now." Billy was through the door before she'd finished the last syllable.

"The children are safe out here?" Lorrie began to worry about that. The Indians at the fort didn't look threatening, but like winter they could sneak up on you, she thought.

"We're near the fort," was all Mrs. Hanson said.

The next morning Billy and Melanie galloped off in different directions after making their final plans; Lorrie heard them discussing routes before they left. Now she looked after them anxiously. "Should they be running the horses like that?" she asked their mother.

"They know how to take care of the horses; they should settle down to a more practical pace soon. And their father will check the horses when they return. Before and after they groom them."

The next few days found people appearing at the Hanson farm with all manner of livestock and food and even cats and dogs. Star and Lorrie had to turn a number of old and sickly animals away, too. Lorrie was tempted by a calico kitten. 'I think Carrol would love it," she told Star. "But is it practical now? When we don't know how much food we'll need?"

Star shook her head. "It might be too early. The cabins are small, and they would be prey. They do like to roam, and they might kill the chicks." Lorrie agreed and reluctantly sent the little girl away with her kitten. The locals were happy to have the chance to make money whenever they could.

The wagon was filling up with basics, cheese, potatoes, bacon and sausage, honey, dried beans, seed corn, and Lorrie even bought a few flowering plants in little pots. Then she bought a baby lilac bush, bread to eat along the way (it wouldn't keep), and two apple tree cuttings. They began turning away more people and livestock; three cows and four pigs should be enough for now. Two days before they planned to leave, they said, "Enough Now!" and began thinking about how to load the pack horse.

Unfortunately, they didn't have enough room for the hay they needed. "Is there any hay for sale?" she asked Mr. Hanson at supper one night. They'd be leaving soon, but she needed to know.

"Lem Jorgeson raises hay for the fort. I don't know what he has. We raise our own."

"Maybe Billy or someone could ask him what he has available. And do you know anyone who could use a yoke or two of oxen? We're going to be short of feed this winter for sure, and we can get along without them. We have a lot of horses."

"I'll ask about the hay and oxen and have word for you if you return, but it's getting late for that," he warned her.

Lorrie was moving bags and barrels again in the wagon trying to make room for everything when a boy rode up on a big black mule. He slid off, hugged the mule's neck and then led it forward. "This is Jake," he announced. "He's not just big and can carry a lot of your supplies, even that crate of chickens, but he's smart. Smarter than most horses, and he's gentle enough to ride."

Lorrie didn't like the way the boy looked so eager and so forlorn. "We'd about decided not to take any more livestock. Too many mouths to feed now." The boy flinched at that.

Star climbed out of the wagon and sat on the seat above them. "You need money really bad, huh?"

Lorrie looked closer at the boy. She hadn't got that. His clothes were clean and mended. Frequently, she saw. "So, how much are you asking?"

"Pa said that twenty five dollars would be a good deal for a mule as good as Jake. He's not just a pack train mule. But I think he's worth at least thirty."

"And your pa's expecting just twenty-five."

The boy got the insinuation before Lorrie did. "I wouldn't lie to my pa. Our family needs that money!" He stood straight and defiant, but his lower lip quivered. The mule moved forward and nuzzled his neck, then looked suspiciously at the two women.

"Maybe he wouldn't be happy with us," Lorrie said softly. "He'd probably run away back to you, and we don't have time to keep that from happening, plus he'd probably spill all the packs when he took off." She shook her head.

"Oh, no," the boy said, shocked. "He'd never do that after I told him not to."

"Quite a paragon," Lorrie said, approaching them both cautiously. "So, what's your name? We could use him, if you can guarantee his behavior. And maybe some time in the future you could buy him back..."

The boy shook his head violently. "No, we're moving back east. Ma says we can't have a mule in town. That he'd be happier out here. She just said that to make me feel better, I know, but maybe it's true. Anyways, my name's Thomas Jamison. You can call me Tommy, and Pa said I should get a receipt."

"Of course, I'll get you your money and make you out a receipt. I've paper and a pencil in my purse. It's too hard to carry pen and ink on the trail. But first you'd better introduce us so that Jake can decide if he wants to stay with us."

The boy nodded. "Yes, I'll have to explain it to him. I didn't before because I didn't know if I'd have to." He was relieved and sorry. "We'll just go over by the other end of the wagon and talk while you get the money—and the receipt."

"What do you think, Star, at least thirty dollars?"

"You've spent a lot here, and you still don't have anywhere near enough feed," Star told her.

Lorrie wasn't happy at the dent all that buying had put in her money belt, but she still had enough for the future, she decided; maybe Jake would be worth thirty. They definitely could use another pack animal.

It was only a few minutes before Tommy came back with Jake close behind him. "I told him that you needed him worse than I did." He looked at the mule, and added, "I've never lied to him." He swallowed, "and we've said our good-byes."

"We do need him, Tommy, as you can see, and we'll take care of him," Star said gently.

"And we'll try to make him happy," Lorrie said. Then she wondered if that sounded silly.

Tommy nodded. "I know. Jake said that you're good people." He swallowed again and walked away with saying anything else, but his head was bent and soon he was running.

Lorrie looked after him. Boys hid their emotions, she'd learned, and so did men, she suspected. "I wouldn't have thought that Jake had known us long enough to think that," she said to Star, and then Jake gave her a firm nudge in her back and when she turned, startled, he nuzzled her hair. "I guess we're going to get along just fine then, huh," and she looked at Star, who was watching them both.

Star giggled, and said to Jake, "Are you ready to be packed?"

The mule moved over to the supplies still sitting on the ground and sniffed them, then looked back at the two women. "Okay, no point dawdling," Lorrie said.

Star packed Jake; she had more experience than Lorrie, and she kept an eye on the mule as she piled more on his back, including a crate of chickens and a smaller crate with a lone duck. Finally, Jake shook his head and stamped a foot, and she shifted the load, removing the duck, which went in the wagon. "I think he's fine with the load now," Star said, and she helped Lorrie finish redistributing the load in the wagon. They tied Lightning and Jake on long lines to the back of the wagon. Star would ride Swift and keep an eye on the wagon and the pack animals. Lorrie didn't notice the troubled glance Star gave her as they packed.

Chapter Seven
~ Returning Home ~

After they finished a lunch of bread and cheese, Lorrie was packing away the food, when Star said, “I didn’t want to worry you before now, but when I went back for more flour, it was an excuse to look around. Two men have been watching us for a couple days now. I probably wouldn’t have noticed them, but one of them laughed and called me a half breed.”

Lorrie hissed. She hadn’t even known what that meant until they’d visited the trading post. “You think they mean trouble?”

“Two lone women with a wagon, horses, and supplies heading down the trail alone could be an invitation to some men.”

Lorrie laughed. “Well, they sure don’t know us. You think it’s only two?”

Star looked at her in surprise. “Pretty sure.”

“So, would they ambush us along the way, or wait until we make camp and are sleeping? That would be easiest for us because we’d be ready. Otherwise one of us has to drive, and the other wait for them, who’d come running back—no time to unpack or unhitch—if she heard a ruckus.”

Star nodded. “I think you’re right. I’ll take Swift off the trail and call out that I have to find some bushes for a few minutes.”

Lorrie smiled. “Now that’s a good plan. I think they’d fall for that invitation, but why should you have all the fun?” And Lorrie remembered her excitement earlier with Bolt; she’d better work at reining her emotions in uncertain situations.

Star was even more surprised. "Can you sneak up on them?"

"Have you ever shot a man?" Lorrie retorted. "I'll wait off the trail and listen. I don't think they'll bother to skulk."

"I'm supposed to be taking care of you," Star protested.

"Nope. I'm supposed to be protecting you. I promised your mother!" Star looked annoyed.

"All right. We'll take turns. After all we don't know when they'll decide to jump us."

"Sounds fair," Lorrie said after considering it. "But I get to go first." She thought the men wouldn't wait, but she saw that Star didn't think Lorrie should have all the responsibility either. She saw Star's point. Friends should share.

They decided to bait their first trap a few miles down the road. If anything happened, the animals could rest after working hard. Lorrie was disappointed when nothing happened. Star took her turn. Again, all was quiet. They kept going longer this time, and closer to dark, Jake shook his head and turned into the team, bringing them to a stop. Lorrie wrapped the reins around the brake and had a sudden suspicion. Grabbing the rifle and bullets for her pistol, she leaped off the wagon and vanished into the bushes. The team waited uneasily.

Star was nowhere to be seen. She'd been a few lengths behind the last time Lorrie had looked back. Had the men grabbed her? Then she heard a man yell as shots rang out. Running back down the trail she came upon Star wrestling with one man while another was on the ground with a wounded arm, but he had a gun aimed at the two struggling figures.

Lorrie decided it was best to take him out before helping Star, but before she could shoot, Jake had burst past her and attacked the man with his teeth, and when Lorrie wrenched her gaze away from him, Star was wiping her knife on her man's shirt.

"Next time it's my turn," Lorrie complained, but she did not enjoy dealing with the bodies. Star dug a rope out of Swift's saddle bag, and they roped the bodies and had Swift drag them to the rocky drop off they'd decided to use after a quick search of the area.

"We'd best throw the saddles down too," Star advised, "though it's a pity to waste them. We'll just turn the horses loose; they may go back to the fort or maybe someone will steal them. That'd be good."

Lorrie nodded. Star had already called Swift in, and they rode double down the trail to the wagon where the horses still waited under Jake's watchful eye. "He's fast," Lorrie commented, "and he didn't lose the pack, though the chickens may never be the same. I'm afraid to look. They're awfully quiet. You did a really good job of packing, though, Star."

"He was careful, I think, but how did he get loose? He must have chewed through the rope."

"Nope," Lorrie replied after she picked the rope up from the ground. "It's still tied to his halter. He untied it from the wagon and must have carried it so he wouldn't step on it. It's awfully wet, and I think there's some blood on it!"

"From the man he finished off. I'm not even sure he needed to stomp him. You know, Tommy was right. We do need Jake more than he did." They looked at the big black mule with more than a little disbelief.

They kept on till almost dark, not wanting to stop too close to what they'd left behind. "Are you going to tell your folks, Star?" Lorrie was curious. She didn't think it was the kind of thing a parent wanted to hear, though she'd been an orphan for a long time. They were eating a light supper of cheese and bread after checking the chickens and letting them out to recover and eat. One staggered a lot, but the others perked up after finding some bugs near a rotted log.

"Yes," Star told her, after some thought. "I think they'll be happy to hear that I can take care of myself."

"You certainly did. And here I was feeling smug and thinking it'd be me 'cause I had the experience."

"I think you're used to rushing in and taking over—maybe," Star mused.

Lorrie looked at her friend. "You think that I'm too headstrong?"

Star looked at her. "You said once—a long time ago—that you missed your uncle. That he'd been taking care of you for a long time. Do you miss that? Being taken care of, I mean."

Lorrie had to stop and think back. "No, I feel free. I never thought that before."

"Just so you're careful when you get that urge, Lorrie. Now I think I'd better lock the chickens back up. We'll flush the crate again in the morning." And they both went to their blankets, mulling over the day and the discussion. And Lorrie told herself once again that she did need to be more cautious before rushing in.

It took longer to return with an overloaded wagon and livestock to herd, but at night, after Jake was unpacked, he herded the livestock and kept them from straying too far. He seemed to enjoy herding them back, they noticed. Several days later they stopped the wagon in front of the Johnson's store to give them some of the supplies they'd brought back for the store. Young George loved the duck so it became his responsibility.

It was Clifford's responsibility to take care of his new little sister, Sarah, who'd been born while they were gone. Elizabeth Johnson bustled up and down the front steps with supplies; and she and Lorrie discussed what seemed fair for the costs of what Lorrie brought back, and Sallie Sue kept records of what they owed her. The whole family was busy and also grateful to have their mother taking care of them instead of all of them taking care of her.

Then Lorrie drove the wagon and the livestock up to their homesteads. Hannah got all the chickens since Evan had built a big coop for them, and Hannah decided which ones would go into the cooking pot. The rest of the cheese, beans, sugar, and other staples were divided between the two cabins since Lorrie would be eating here and there.

Star took Lightning home packed with supplies. "You've earned them," Lorrie said, "and just think how pleased your folks will be to have more supplies for the winter." Lorrie had bought a number of trade blankets for winter and shared them with each home. Most of her furniture and supplies were under the big wagon's canvas. She looked forward to having them safe under her roof, though they'd be moved inside wherever there was room in another cabin or at the Johnson's when it had its second story.

After unloading, she visited each home to look at its progress. The Browns' cabin's root cellar was finished and lined with stone that the oxen had hauled down from the rocky slopes. The walls were up and the roof nearly finished. Evan was concentrating on shingles now for all the roofs. Their lean-to was ready for the livestock, though it would be snug, but all the warmer for that. Hannah spent a lot of her time chinking.

The Michaels' house/barn was finished, the roof up, and the loft snug for supplies. Dennis had decided to use a stall for his room, and he'd started on a cellar in hopes of getting it dug before the ground froze. The Johnsons' second story was started, and they hoped to finish it before winter, and they'd started on a barn for their stock and hay. It was almost October, and the men worked from house to house to barn as the women harvested and canned. Brock Summers announced one day that his winter preparations were finished, and he helped build. The three wood stoves for heating and cooking were divided among the three homes, though the Michaels' was stored at the Johnson's; Lorrie knew she'd have to be satisfied with a fireplace until she could find another stove. Still, a fireplace sounded good, since it meant that she'd have a house to put it in—someday.

Chapter Eight
~ Return to Fort Laramie in Winter ~

A lot of the food Lorrie'd brought back from the fort was stored in the Brown's cellar; some went up in the Michaels' loft, but most had to be taken back down to the Johnson's General Store. "Sallie Sue is keeping track of all your supplies," Elizabeth reassured Lorrie, as she stood in the kitchen bracing baby Sarah on one hip while she used her other hand to stir the soup she was making for supper. "And Sam is going to make a sign for the store this winter. He has boards curing. Mr. Summers says that we'll be doing a lot of chinking when the logs shrink, but we should be all right this winter, and we'll have to stop building for a bit to hay so we have enough for the animals." She frowned. "I'll be glad when winter's over," she confessed. "We'll have a whole season to get ready for the next one."

Lorrie nodded. "You're snug here, though, and we can butcher the livestock if we have to."

"Not the cows!"

"Oh, probably not." It was Lorrie's turn to reassure her, but then she went out on the front porch and looked at the colorful trees covering the valley's wide slopes. Beautiful, but not a good sign. It was time for her to get back to work.

For a change, she rode Sunny up to the Summers' cabin. She needed the exercise, and if she rode Shadow on the trail, she wanted her to be fresh. But why ride Shadow or Sunny. She'd be driving the oxen, and she could ride Jake if she needed to ride and leave the horses to graze and work. Of course, she planned to take the small wagon too so there'd be enough room for any hay she could purchase. Now she just needed a companion.

Star was saddling Swift when Lorrie arrived. She looked up and came quickly to meet her. "You're planning to go back for hay, aren't you? I thought you would, but Mother says that she needs me here, to gather the roots and berries from the woods, and help her tan hides. I think she's afraid of the weather, but Father says it's her decision. I'm sorry. I was looking forward to going with you again, but Mother saw me looking at my winter clothes, and became suspicious. I didn't say anything to them yet, because I didn't want them to worry." She sighed.

Lorrie was dismayed. "How close is winter? Do they know?"

"No, not yet, but a blizzard can come up fast. If you're going, you have to go now. That I do know."

Lorrie didn't sigh, though she was tempted. She'd take Carrol if Dennis would let her go. Before long she was down at the Michaels' barn. Carrol had given up calling it a house because it would obviously be too small with the new cows and pigs. She had even helped her brother and the men finish digging the cellar, and now all the men were preparing logs, while Evan made more shingles. The well would be next, though possibly the next year. Meanwhile they hauled water up from the river.

She was peeling potatoes when Lorrie arrived, so Lorrie joined her on one of the rocks they'd gathered for the foundation. "I have to start for the hay now," she said, "and Star can't go. I need another driver for the second wagon. Even Jake can't do that," and she laughed, but glanced sideways at Carrol.

Carrol put the potato and knife in the bowl at her side. "You're asking me? I'd love to go, but I knew you'd rather have Star, because she can fight better than I can."

"You've never tried, and Dennis won't want you to go, but I don't want to ask any of the men. Those logs are heavy, and women should only do the light work."

Carrol stared at her. "Oh, you're joking," though she wasn't sure. "When are you going?"

"As soon as I can hitch them up. I'm not asking or telling anyone. I've wasted enough time. Brock has scared me silly, but we need that hay as soon as possible. I can't wait. As a matter of fact I'm leaving today because I don't want to wake up to snow."

Carrol nodded. “All the animals are down in the valley grazing, and it’s good that we’re keeping the wagons down by the Johnson’s for storage unless we need them. You hitch up the oxen and start off. You’re probably already packed?” Lorrie nodded. “I have to finish chores here and pack, and then I’ll ride Firefly to the Johnson’s and leave her in their corral and hitch up Shadow and Sunny to the small wagon and catch up with you. They’re faster than the oxen so that will work. I will not waste time discussing it with Dennis,” she said defiantly.

“Okey dokey. I’m on my way.” Lorrie rode Sunny to the Johnson’s and left her in the corral for Carrol after rounding up the oxen and herding them to the big wagon. She loaded her pack in the big wagon—just in case Carrol couldn’t make it. She hoped she wouldn’t run into Dennis. She called Jake in and put the pack saddle on him. It was a good thing almost everything she owned was at the Johnson’s.

After harnessing the oxen and getting them moving, she stopped in front of the general store and left Jake watching the oxen. She didn’t find Elizabeth, but George was on the back porch. He was peeling potatoes too, she noticed. “Mother took Sarah up to see Hannah,” he told her. “She didn’t like the way she was spitting up, and she didn’t want to ask Hannah to come down when she’s busy. And I think she likes riding now that she can,” he confided.

“That’s all right,” Lorrie said, relieved. “Tell her good-bye for me. We’re off again.”

George wasn’t surprised. Lorrie was off every chance she could, he’d noticed. “Have a fun trip. Oh, and maybe you could bring me back a puppy sometime,” he added hopefully.

“Maybe next year,” was all she’d promise, and she climbed up on the wagon seat and started the oxen off. They’d make good time with an empty wagon, she thought, and she’d taken all her blankets, just in case, plus the furs that Star had given her. Jake trotted alongside, unless he decided to hang behind or forge ahead. She didn’t worry about him anymore.

Lorrie was wondering whether to fret or not when she heard the jangling of horses’ harness coming up behind her. “Sorry I’m late,” Carrol called to her, “but Dennis came home, and I had to send him on an errand up to the Summers’. That’s as far as I could think to send him. Then I raced Firefly to the Johnson’s, paid George to rub her down, and left a note for Dennis with him. I told him not to dare leave our house ’til it was finished!"

"Oh, well done," Lorrie called back. Later, when the trail widened, she let Carrol take the horses ahead so the oxen could take their time and maybe be encouraged to keep up. After Jake checked out Sunny and Shadow, he took the lead.

They were a couple days out from Fort Laramie, Lorrie was pretty sure, when they woke up one morning to a definite nip in the air. "Star, her mother, and Brock could tell us what that means," she said to Carrol, "but to me it just means we'd better make better time."

It had warmed up by the time they reached the Hanson's, but Lorrie knew better than to be reassured. It merely made her worry more. She was relieved when Mr. Hanson came out of the house before she'd climbed down from the wagon. "Well, I wasn't sure you'd come back," he told her, "though I knew you really wanted that hay. Jorgenson has saved some for you in case he can get a better price than at the fort. And Matthew Carstairs, also known as Old Slick, is interested in your oxen. But stand your ground with him because he wants everything cheap as he can get it. I'll tell Billy to have him meet us at the Jorgenson's to look them over."

"Thank you, Mr. Hanson, I appreciate your help. 'Course I have to use the oxen to get the hay home, but I'll bring them back as soon as I can."

Jorgenson's men were loading the wagons with hay when Carstairs arrived. He studied the oxen for a while, then said, "I see you're loading them up. Why's that?" He had black hair slicked back and a sleek black mustache, but Lorrie didn't think that was why he was called Slick.

Lorrie blinked at him a couple times, then said with some surprise. "We have to use them to take the hay home. Then I'll bring them back."

"Huh, they won't be worth as much then." It didn't seem to bother him. Instead he seemed quite cheerful. Lorrie was glad that Hanson had warned her.

She sighed and shook her head. "You can decide if you want them when we come back then." She brightened. "But they're good stock and haven't been working much lately. I think you'll want them."

He grunted and shook his head. "Tell me when you're back, and I'll see if they're worth anything." She was pretty sure he was smiling when he left.

She shrugged and said to herself, Maybe I'll keep them. But then she heard a gentle cough behind her, and turned to see a man emerging from the Jorgenson's big barn. He was shorter and grayer than Old Slick, and Lorrie wondered what he wanted.

"No need to let him see me," he remarked to them generally. "Billy dropped by my place after he stopped at Carstairs'. He said that maybe I'd like to take a look too. He doesn't like Carstairs much 'cause of what he's heard from Jerry, his best friend, and Carstairs' youngest."

"So, are you interested? One yoke or two?"

"Just one pair. I like the red and whites."

"They're Jemmy and Dolly. Jemmy has the most red. But they're all sweet-tempered and hard workers. I'd keep them if it weren't for feeding them,"

Jogenson had been watching the hay being loaded, but he'd moved closer when Carstairs arrived to observe the haggling. "I might be interested in the other pair," he told Lorrie. "I can use them for hauling to spell my other teams. And I'm fine with you using them and bringing them back, though I'm wondering when that will be."

"As soon as possible," she promised, "and I am keeping an eye on the weather."

"Just so you pay attention and don't take foolish chances."

Carrol gave a smothered snort, but said, "I think it's the hay dust," when they turned to look at her.

"I think we should give the ladies a down payment, Joe, to be sure Old Slick can't shove his way in. And this is Joseph Wallace, an old friend from a ways out. Billy must have made good time, Joe," Jorgenson said curiously.

"It's possible he came to my place first. Just possible, and then I might have lent him a fresh horse. His is behind the barn," and Wallace smiled.

Lorrie was glad to take the down payments, and she and Carrol left as soon as the hay had been loaded in the two wagons and covered with the wagon canvas. It was slower going with full wagons, and three days down the road, snowflakes began drifting down and melting on the oxen's backs, Lorrie saw with dismay. "Do we stop?" Carrol called back to her.

"No," Lorrie decided. "The closer we are to home, the better. We'll stop when we have to." The snow accumulated slowly, and they were able to keep going 'til almost dark. In the morning, while they ate breakfast, the sun came out and the snow melted.

"It's a good thing the ground is harder, so melting snow won't make it muddy. We start now and go as long as possible, but we won't hurry the animals. We'll watch to see when they get tired."

"That sounds smart," Carrol agreed, "but I'm sure glad it melted, and it's warming up faster, I think." The weather held, and the hay was forked into all three barns, including the Michaels', the day after they returned.

Carrol looked with satisfaction at her house, which was taking shape. "Thanks Dennis, for not leaving the building. Do you think we can move in soon? I was afraid we'd have to sleep on hay in our loft."

Dennis looked at his sister with some annoyance. "I would have stayed awake at night worrying if I weren't so tired, and I did want to surprise you." His tone softened. "I'm glad you went and brought back the hay 'cause I worried about feeding the animals too."

"We do have a lot of livestock to feed. I don't think this is enough. We'll probably have to butcher some of the cows," Lorrie said. She'd stayed with Carrol in case her brother came down too hard on her. Now she could relax and plan her next trip. The oxen definitely had to go back straightaway.

Lorrie left before first light the next morning. She didn't ask anyone to go with her. She'd make good time with no wagons, and she'd take Jake to ride back. She felt safer with him than Sunny or Shadow. They were good horses, broke both for riding and pulling, but mules were survivors. And she could pack Jake with supplies and the small canvas, along with a few short poles, in case she needed a tent.

This time the snow started before she'd been two days on the trail. It didn't stop, and it got colder and colder. She stopped the oxen when Jake stood still and stood with his back to the wind. "Now's the time, huh. Good boy." And she made the oxen lie down; next to them she struggled to put the canvas up. Finally, she gave in and braced the poles into a teepee shape; it was more practical and quicker. She tried to get Jake inside for warmth, but he stayed out with the oxen, and she wrapped herself in blankets and buffalo hides. She kept the food inside next to her body so it wouldn't freeze.

After that she slept and ate and thought about going outside to relieve herself, but the tent was partially buried, and she couldn't dig herself out. Finally she woke up coughing because it was hard to breathe.

She felt stifled, and the only thing she could think of to do was call for help. “Come, Jake,” she called out twice, before she realized that she was merely whispering, so she hit on the tent walls and pushed against them for a few minutes before she had to rest. I’m glad I didn’t bring anyone with me, she thought, and they’ve got hay and one less mouth to feed. You don’t have to do it all, she remembered Hannah telling her. Okay, Hannah, she whispered. You’re right. I’ll rest now, and she laid her head down.

The next thing she knew there was snow and fresh air on her face, and Jake had the canvas in his teeth and was still pulling it away so that the one side was open. “I forgot how good you were with your teeth,” she exclaimed, and hugged his warm body after pushing herself up. “Good Jake. It’s all right; I can take the tent down by myself now.” She saw that it had stopped snowing, and while it felt pretty cold, she said to Jake, “It’s just brisk. We’re ready to go.” And then she remembered the oxen.

There were four hills close to the tent, and steam rose now and then in little puffs. She dug with her hands, warm in the fur-lined gloves Many Stars had given her when she returned safely with Star. She dug carefully where the muzzle should be, and soon a pair of gentle, brown eyes gazed at her. The ox shook its head free of the snow and heaved itself to its feet; it was Dolly, and before long three more hills erupted, and all four oxen began grazing on the grass that appeared where their warm bodies had lain.

Lorrie sat down on the pile of canvas and ate her own meal. Afterwards, she struggled again with the canvas. It was stiff from the cold, and she had to tie it and the poles in a tangled mass behind Jake’s saddle. He looked at her once, but she said, “I’m almost done. We can go soon.” She hoped it wouldn’t fall off; if it did, she’d leave it. And then she had Jake herd the oxen back along the trail.

Well, there used to be a trail. Now it was buried under the snow. I should have learned some good curse words, she thought in alarm. Then she patted the mule’s neck and said, “We have to go to the fort, Jake. Where the hay is.” He waited patiently for her to make sense.

“Good heavens, girl,” she scolded herself aloud. “You know what direction it’s in, and it doesn’t matter if the trail’s covered. You have to go while you can still have the sun to guide you.” So she kept moving until dark, gave up on making a tent and curled up between two oxen.

Their warm breath on her was the last thing she felt before she went to sleep.

She woke up with the sun in her eyes, and gave thanks. All the animals were up and pawing through the snow to get at the grass. She let them eat while keeping an eye on the sun, and when they moved away from the open area and began relieving themselves, she started them towards the fort again.

Lorrie had no idea how far out she still was. She certainly wasn't aware of the day because she'd lost track of time, but in a couple days she began coming across tracks. Some were sleigh tracks, she thought, and it wasn't long before she spotted ranch buildings in the distance. Must be the Hanson's, she thought. They were closest to the trail, which is why she'd chosen to stop there the first time.

* * * *

She stopped Jake at the hitching rack in front of the house and was wondering if she should put the oxen in the big corral, when Billy burst out of the front door, dressed only in trousers and a shirt. "You're here," he yelled. "I wondered if you was still coming. Ma said that you'd have enough sense to stay home, but Pa said, Maybe not."

Lorrie laughed and felt safe. She was glad she came. "Will you ask your pa where I should put the stock and can someone tell Mr. Jorgenson and Mr. Wallace that we're here?"

"I'll ask him. I'll be right out."

"Put on a jacket first," she called after him.

"Get in the house and warm up, Miss Lorrie," Johann Hanson said as he came out, buttoning his coat. "And there's some breakfast for you. How was your journey? Where did you sleep?" He came over to Jake and looked at the tangled mess on his back. "What's that?" he asked her.

"My tent. I camped out, but I couldn't roll it up again afterwards."

"Bring it in the house. We'll warm it up by the stove."

"Jake'll appreciate that. I tried to keep it from rubbing on him."

"Unload your pack here, and put him in the corral with the oxen, and go on in to break your fast."

Lorrie unloaded her pack on the porch, and Hanson carried it inside. When he came back out, she had Jake in the corral and was checking on the water trough to see if it was frozen. "Can I give him some of your hay?" she called back, after ascertaining that the ice had been broken in the trough.

"Help yourself," he said and joined her. "You've got some credit here."

Later, after Lorrie had appreciatively eaten a hot breakfast, she sat as close to the stove as she could, sitting on the floor because all the chairs were too far away. She had moved to a chair but had a blanket draped around her that Mrs. Hanson had given her when Jorgenson arrived.

"I stopped at the corral," he told her. "They all look good."

"They had nothing to pull coming back, but grazing was sparse," she said.

He nodded. "How far up the trail were you before it ran out?"

"Two days. Then we camped for a while."

"There's her tent over by the stove, Lem," and Hanson pointed at it.

Jorgenson studied it. It wasn't as stiff now, and he pulled it apart to study it closer. "Looks like teeth marks here," he remarked, pointing at the tear marks.

Hanson moved over and squatted down to look. "I didn't notice it before. When did that happen, Miss Lorrie?"

"When Jake pulled it off me. It got buried in the snow."

The two men looked at her. "Mules are smart," Jorgenson said. Lorrie nodded and pulled the blanket closer.

Later in the afternoon, Wallace arrived. He, too, stopped at the corral to check the oxen before going to the house. "They're looking good, ma'am. In pretty near the same shape as when they were here last."

Lorrie smiled, but before she could say anything, Hanson said, "They weren't pulling anything on the way back, but the grazing was sparse."

"That explains it," Wallace said, but he knew he was missing something. "So when did you get here. Before the blizzard? You waited until now to send for me?"

"Nope, Joe. She just got here. She had to camp out on the trail."

Wallace glanced from Hanson to Lorrie. "That was some blizzard. I'm glad you got here safe. I've brought the money, and I think that the price we agreed on still holds. I brought a receipt. You'll excuse my hurry, I hope, but I do want to get back before the next blizzard."

Lorrie stood up. "How soon? I have to get back!"

Mrs. Hanson had been standing in the kitchen doorway. "No. We can't let you go without a warm night's sleep and plenty of hot food.

And we'll see if the weather holds in the morning," she said firmly.

Lorrie hesitated, and they all looked at her and frowned. She flushed. "I'm not stupid. I'll stay the night. And thank you all." Thinking about it later, after she had been tucked into bed by Mrs. Hanson, who made sure the blankets were wrapped around Lorrie, she was grateful. No matter what happened on the trip home, she'd be better off with plenty of food to fortify her. And so would Jake. And she was grateful that she'd replenished her money supply and gotten rid of the oxen, though she'd miss them. They'd been useful on the trail and in the settlement, and they had better homes than they'd have had with Carstairs, she was sure.

The ride home was uneventful, though she paid more attention to the sky and the landmarks than she ever had. Mr. Hanson had rolled the canvas up for her and given her a hide tent for the return trip. "Keep it," he told her as he added it to Jake's pack. "I wouldn't want to think of you ever again having to use that wagon canvas as a tent."

Lorrie was feeling warm from her stop, both for the warm respite and the friends she'd made, and she kept Jake moving at a good pace so she'd be as close to home as possible if another storm struck. The return trip was clear, however, though cold, and when she got to the Michaels' cabin, it was almost finished. The last shingle was hammered in two weeks before the next blizzard. Evan looked up the sky and said, "Thank you, Lord," before everyone scattered to their homes to finish last minute chores as the first flake drifted lazily to the ground.

Chapter Nine
~ Spring is Sprung ~

"Spring is sprung, the grass is riz, I wonder where the flowers is," George sang as he splashed through the mud heading for the barn. Lorrie smiled. She was high and dry on the Johnson's front porch where she'd jumped from Sunny's back. The horse and Jake were looking for grass now farther up the valley.

"George has sure grown in just a little while," she said to Elizabeth Johnson, who'd joined her on the porch.

"And Sarah'll be walking before too long." The older woman looked at Lorrie and added, "We made it through the winter, thanks to you, girl, and we've still got enough food. And I'm pleased as punch that we did not go on to Oregon Territory."

"Winter is still hanging around, Brock said. March is too soon to plant. We have a few wisps of hay left, but I'm sorry we ran out of grain for the livestock. Still, butchering those two cows helped out." Lorrie shook her head regretfully. She'd worked hard to get those cows.

"What we really need now is flour," Elizabeth said. "Along with sugar. The honey helped out, but I do want some sugar. Actually I'm making a list of all the things we need in case you want to bring in more supplies." She looked hopefully at Lorrie. "It's not just for us, but I'd like to stock the store too," she admitted.

Lorrie nodded. "I know. I have a list of things I want for my cabin when it's built. The ground's too hard for digging still. I do want a cellar. At least I've got all the pots and dishes and furniture I need. I'm glad you had room to store them."

Elizabeth smiled. “Plenty of room, and when you have your home, we’ll use that space for the store. Sam’s been making shelves and building a counter. He finished the sign already. Uh, are you thinking of going back to the fort?”

Lorrie shook her head. “I’m thinking of going straight to the source, maybe back to Missouri and hiring a pack train. I expect to find more than just the basics there.”

“Maybe some cheese? At least we have plenty of meat. Who you planning to take this time?”

“Dennis. A man might come in handy back there. And it’s early enough not to need him here for planting and digging. What do you think?”

“Sounds like a good idea, though I’m surprised you’re admitting you need a man.”

Lorrie grinned. “I’m also thinking of giving him the chance to meet other people. You know, girls. We don’t have a lot of choice here, and Carrol said something the other day about maybe bringing in new settlers now that we’re established. Be sure to stake out your home site that you spoke of a while back.”

“I want bricks.”

“Plenty of clay by the river, I think, and we can float supplies in maybe some time. We need masons and mills too. I’ll be looking for more than supplies.”

“You’re right. I’m surprised you’re still here.”

“I haven’t talked to Dennis or Carrol yet. Just thinking about it.” She whistled, and Jake trotted up with Sunny, nudging the mare close to the porch so Lorrie could climb back on. Lorrie took time to stop by her home site. There were plenty of logs curing to one side, and rocks marked the corners of her cabin. She would have front and back porches, a barn, a well and… That’s enough to start with, she told herself, looking at the trees that had yet to come down to make room for her garden.

From there she rode straight to the Michaels cabin, where the brother and sister sat on the porch. Carrol was looking disconsolately at the mud. “What’s wrong?” Lorrie asked.

Dennis laughed. “The ground’s too hard for digging. I almost broke a shovel showing her that. Not that I want to dig in the mud anyways.”

Carrol tossed her red hair back. “You don’t know until you try,” she told them. “I’ll have lunch in a little while, Lorrie. Want to bring me some canned tomatoes from the cellar? I've got bread rising."

"I thought we were almost out of flour," Lorrie said in pleased surprise.

"We are now. No point in waiting for the weevils."

"A good meal will be welcome," Lorrie said, "before I hit the trail." The red-headed pair stared at her. "You know we need supplies, and I think more seed too."

"Who's going with you?" Carrol asked hopefully. You didn't have to do the tedious, daily chores on the trail.

"I'm thinking of asking Dennis," Lorrie said, studying him.

He straightened. He topped his sister by about half a foot, and now he looked taller. "Both wagons? You need another driver?"

"Nope. I'm thinking of hiring a pack train back down the trail, possibly all the way to Independence. The trail's probably going to be mud for a month or more, Brock said. And the wagons will be needed for hauling here, especially since it's time to finish cleaning out the barns and the manure piles and scatter it on the fields before planting."

"So I get to clean out the barn," Carrol said, not trying to hide her disappointment.

Dennis shook his head. "'Course not, sis. I'll start shoveling it out after lunch. I'll check Pewter's tack first."

"I'll start on lunch now," Carrol said. "I know Lorrie doesn't hang around long once she's made up her mind."

After Dennis went whistling off to the barn, Lorrie turned to Carrol. "Remember what you were saying the other day about needing fresh blood? Well, this will be his chance to meet someone and maybe bring her back. I'll be looking for fresh faces too."

"A man? Are you going to look up Bolt?"

"The thought crossed my mind, though he didn't seem the settling down type, and he didn't really pay much attention to me. In any case, I want a few more settlers at least. It's too early for a wagon train. I might scout them out later."

"We need to stake our claims before anyone new comes," Carrol said, suddenly worried.

"That's another thing I'll be checking out," Lorrie told her. "I have no idea when we'll be back, but for staking claims, I thought a man might be necessary. I almost got sent back home because I was a lone woman. Oh, that seems like years ago," she said thinking back and remembering her frustration. She had wanted to slap that wagon master.

"You're right. I see that now," Carrol admitted. "And I was thinking of having a house in town. If Dennis ever brings home a bride, it won't be my home any longer," and she frowned, thinking of the hard labor she'd put into her cabin.

"Stake it out now," Lorrie'd advised. "And we also need to decide on plots for a school and a church. Maybe you can work with Elizabeth on that decision. She should have some say in that!"

They didn't leave until the next morning, because Lorrie had learned the wisdom of a good warm and dry sleep and a hot meal before setting out. They drifted through Lotawater about midday and went on to Wayside. Lorrie planned to look up Timmy, Jason, and Bolt, but the boys found her first. Not surprised, she shook their hands. They were taller and broader, also even more confident, and they shook hands with Dennis, too.

"First of all, I want to thank you for the two chickens. They're good layers, and were never even considered for the stew pot. I named them Tammy and Jenny."

Jason got it first. "You named them after us!" Timmy looked at him in surprise. "Well, sorta," Jason told him. Then he looked steadily at Lorrie. "The marshal's outta town," he told her. "And, uh, he's courting the new schoolmarm." They both looked worriedly at her.

"Well, she is one lucky woman," she told them, smiling at them after a few seconds thought. "We're moving on down the trail tomorrow, but be sure to give him my regards." She saw the relief on their faces and grinned. "Anything new here, other than that?"

Jason took her query seriously. "The town off by the old mill by Rocky Falls has a newspaper, they say, that covers the whole territory. I haven't seen it myself, but the man came through town and said our town would get copies."

"Do you give him news?"

"Give him news? Why?" Jason was curious; he scented an opportunity.

"Newspapers need news. They have reporters sometimes, and people give them news."

"Do they pay?"

"Maybe. You'll have to ask, but you have the chance to hear things about who's doing what to whom. What the Ladies' Aid is doing. Stuff like that."

"What's a Ladies' Aid?"

"Reporters have to learn these things," she told them.

Jason nodded. "We will," he promised her.

Lorrie decided that it would be interesting to stop at Rocky Falls on the way, and they were directed to the newspaper office, where they heard the heavy, slamming sound of a printing press and a man cursing. The man at the printing press was tall and stocky, but he looked strong. Probably from wrestling with the printing press, Lorrie surmised.

He straightened up and brightened, she was pretty sure, though it was hard to tell with the ink smeared on his face, hands, and apron. "Come in, come in," he told them. "Welcome to Territory Tales. Can I sell you a paper or do you have news for me?" Dennis had started to put out his hand, but decided against it. The man laughed and introduced himself. "Wilson Matthews, but call me Ink. Everyone does."

"Dennis Michaels and my aunt, Lorena Emerson," Dennis said formally. The three had early on decided to keep the family relationship they'd formed on the trail, and it was better for traveling now.

"We heard about your paper," Lorrie said, "and I thought you're a man who's probably on top of the news and who's making it. Do you know where I, that is, we, can hire a pack train? And is there an official in charge of registering claims herabouts?"

"I know just the man for the mule train. He brought my printing press up here—in pieces, of course, but some of those mules still walk funny. And I'll direct you to the nearest authority. He helped me with my paperwork."

"Thanks," Lorrie said gratefully. "I was hoping we wouldn't have to go too far afield."

Ink suddenly frowned. "Sounds like you're not sticking to the beaten path then."

"Not so much. We don't have wagons this time. Why?"

"People tell me things for various reasons, and one of the things I heard is that on a little used trail north of here is an old way station. The main trail moved south, but there's what's apparently a boarding house now. Rumor has it that wayfarers have stopped there and never been seen again. No sign at all."

"What about the sheriff of Rocky Falls?"

"It seems he's a cousin of the owner. Oh, he went there, they say, after a few people complained, but came back to town, and said there's no proof of wrong-doing." Ink shrugged. "Maybe there wasn't any proof. But Mrs. Collins is still wondering about her missing son. He was coming from that direction, and he'd been mining."

Lorrie stared hard at the floor. Bullies and bandits, she thought. Someone should take care of them. She looked up at Ink finally. "Uh, where is it? So we can avoid it?"

Dennis looked at her, and his eyes widened. He swallowed. "We'll definitely keep away, sir. Thank you for the warning."

"Can you draw me a map?" Lorrie asked. She was smiling.

"Is there a good hotel nearby?" Dennis asked. "With good hot food. We like to be prepared before setting out." Ink nodded and drew them two little maps.

Outside Territory Tales, Dennis swung up into the saddle, and Lorrie mounted Shadow. She rode Sunny sometimes to exercise her, but on the trail Shadow had the better gait for easy riding. Jake trailed behind on a long line. In town Lorrie preferred to have him behave like an ordinary mule, not like a dog that ran loose. They rode slowly toward the hotel at the other end of the street. The sign said Tucker's Saloon.

Inside it actually was a hotel with a bar to one side. Dennis asked for two rooms side by side. "My aunt's nervous in towns," Dennis told the leering man. He was glad that Lorrie hadn't seen the clerk's knowing expression.

Upstairs Dennis dropped Lorrie's pack on the bed. He'd refused to let her carry it up. "So. Tell me now if you're planning something."

Lorrie didn't waste time trying to fool him. "If they're innocent, we'll only have been off the trail a little while, and you never can tell what we might find—that we need, I mean. And if they're bad, they shouldn't be allowed to get away with it."

Dennis wanted to argue, but he knew it wouldn't do any good, and he remembered her actions when they'd met. He couldn't say, Well, you saved us, but you can't help anyone else.

They left early the next morning, heading in the opposite direction, then circled around well beyond the town. They kept the horses to a steady pace, and Jake followed behind since there was no trail. They stopped to let the horses graze whenever they came across some early grass, and they reached the ramshackle building before dark.

Lorrie let Dennis register, interrupting only to be sure that their room was clean with fresh bedding and to ask about supper. Soon they followed the smell of steak and fried potatoes to the dining room. Two places were set, and Lorrie looked at the food and sighed. Dennis pulled her chair out, and she sat down, but when he lifted his fork, she jumped up and took it away from him. Then she hugged him around his neck and said, "Let's eat in our room. We'll have a picnic! Can we do that, mister?" She looked at the man with the gray and greasy beard who'd served them. "I promise not to get food on the blankets. Oh, Dennis, this will be so much fun. I don't want to wait!" She put a lot of emphasis on the wait.

She did make their server put their food on a tray and carry it up for them. When he put it on the old dresser, she clapped her hands in glee and stood by the open door to encourage him to leave. Then she closed and locked the door. "Unfortunately, we can't eat it. It could be poisoned," she explained to Dennis. And, of course, they'll have keys. If I'd thought of this sooner, I'd have brought some cheese and jerky from our packs. I'm going to be really hungry in the morning."

Dennis saw that she was chattering to relieve the tension, and he looked at the bed. "So that's why you wanted one room. I should have guessed, but you had the bit in your teeth, and I had to let you run."

She nodded. "Want to take turns jumping up and down on the bed?"

He looked at her in surprise and then blushed. "I'm not going to do the moaning and groaning, I swear!"

"Just grunt. A lot of men do that, or so I'm told. Then we'll go to bed early 'cause we're really tired; we'll have to keep watch." Lorrie was keyed up. She hoped they wouldn't have to wait long, but she remembered that she couldn't get too excited. This wasn't a game or a hunting trip. Not exactly, anyway.

After Dennis' first tentative jump, the bed squeaked and rocked. "I don't think it can take much activity," he told her. And blushed again.

She nodded and studied the walls, the dresser, the floor, and the bed carefully. "No bullet holes," she said thoughtfully. "Well, there wouldn't be, would there?"

"Why not?"

"Proof," she said. "They'd have to be careful."

"The poison would be a good idea," he said, looking regretfully at the congealing food.

"I think they'll have backup. I would. There appears to be only one door. Check the walls." They examined all the walls, and Dennis crawled along the floor and peeked under the bed too. "I think one of us should be on each side of the door; we'll have to be careful not to shoot each other."

He was tempted to ask her if she was as confident as she sounded, but decided against it. "I think I'll lie down for a while." Then he looked at the bed suspiciously. "Is it safe?"

"I don't know. Good question. The bedclothes should be safe," she added doubtfully, pulling them carefully off the bed. They split the blankets between them and put out the lamp.

Lorrie listened with one ear on the floor. She also listened for Dennis snoring, but he was quiet. Maybe he didn't snore. Would the men be listening too? She hadn't thought to tell him to snore. Then she heard a loud snore. Was that real? Was he pretending? She was tempted to crawl over to him to check, but she didn't want to be caught off guard. Then she heard a slight squeak outside the door, followed by a shushing whisper.

She had put her two guns on the blanket; now she picked them up carefully. They were already cocked. She hadn't wanted to make any suspicious noises when they came. She hoped Dennis was awake.

The door eased open, and there was a gleam of light from a dark lantern. Shoot. The bedclothes should be piled on the bed. The light shone on the bed, and a man said, "What the hell?!"

"You lost?" Dennis asked, and Lorrie saw the gleam of a knife as the intruder went for him. Then a light shone on her, and another man grabbed for her. She threw herself backward and pulled the trigger. "The man cursed, but it didn't sound like a wounded curse. There was a struggle on her right, so she shot again upwards. This time a man cried out, and he fell on her. The light was brighter now; they wanted to see what was happening, and so did she.

Three men were in the room, and one had Dennis by the throat; he'd dropped his knife to go for the gun in Dennis' hand. She rolled from under the wounded man's body as he shoved himself away. The man holding the light raised it; he planned to bash her head in, she realized, and shot him. He fell back out the door, and she looked to see how Dennis was doing, just as he brought his knee up and shot the man on top of him as he went backward, then he turned his gun towards Lorrie and shot the man who had his knife at her throat. She'd lost track of him and let him get behind her. She needed practice, she thought dizzily.

She was still sitting on the floor when Dennis opened the dark lantern completely. “You all right?” he asked, kneeling beside her.

“Yes, I was a little dizzy for a second. Everything happened so fast! And I was afraid you were asleep.”

“Did you really think I’d let you down?” he demanded. “You think you have to do everything yourself?”

“Why do people keep saying that?” she demanded of the room at large.

“Let’s pack and get out of here,” he recommended. “Are you planning to report this to the sheriff? Somehow that thought makes me nervous.” She shook her head. “Did he go after you with a knife too? I didn’t see another one.” He flashed the light around the room. He stopped with the light shining on pieces of rope by the door. “My God, I don’t think they were going to kill you.”

“Not yet, anyway,” and she shivered. She’d better spend more time thinking before she did something like this again.

They were halfway down the stairs when they heard a man scream from outside. Dennis beat Lorrie to the door, but only because he was in the lead. In the dirt front yard, a man was running from the stable, bloody knife in hand; it glinted in the moonlight that bathed the scene. He was dragging one leg as he headed toward the house; he saw them on the porch and stopped. It was a fatal mistake for in less than a minute Jake succeeded in kicking down the door the man had bolted behind him, and in less time than that Jake had knocked him down and turned back to stomp him, but the man was sprawled on his back with the knife sticking out of his chest.

“Off, Jake. Enough! Leave it!” To Lorrie’s relief the mule listened to her, sniffed the body and ran back into the stable.

“Jake looked fine,” Dennis said. “He must have cut one of the horses with that knife,” and he ran into the stable after Jake.

Dennis was examining Pewter by the light of another dark lantern when she came in. “Looks like he was going for her throat,” Dennis said. “It’s not a bad cut, and it’s already stopped bleeding. He went for her first ’cause Shadow was harder to see, and Jake wouldn’t have let him near him. Good thing he was on guard here. I’m surprised he wasn’t locked in a stall.”

“Oh, he probably was,” Lorrie told him, “but look at the bolt. That’s nothing for Jake."

Dennis looked at the bolt and nodded, "Firefly would have had that open in a minute too," he told her.

They were leading the horses out of the barn when Lorrie stopped and looked back. "Why would they kill the horses there and not in the woods?'

Dennis looked back at the barn too. "Because it was close to where they were going to dispose of the bodies."

"I don't see how… A horse, after all. It would have to be very close." She frowned "I'm not going to look, but who will we tell? I don't plan to spend time here explaining anything."

"How could we?!" he demanded.

"We could leave a clue there."

"There's Pewter's blood."

"Too easy to miss that, but maybe a hint of treasure. They must have stolen lots over the years."

"You just said that we're not going to look."

Lorrie swallowed. "Something from the bodies maybe. Money, a watch…" She looked back at the house and shuddered.

Dennis looked at her sympathetically. "I'll look, and what you should do is start covering our tracks. They're all over the yard and path here. I'll cut some branches."

Lorrie led the horses up the trail, telling Jake to stay close and guard them. Then she began brushing the tracks that led from the house to the barn. She was on her way up the trail, when Dennis came up behind her swishing his branch back and forth.

"I found two pocket watches and several gold coins on the bodies and left them on the floor where Pewter was standing. That should make them hunt."

"If no one steals them first," she worried.

He shrugged. "Can't do anything about that. It'd be best if there were a crowd."

She agreed. Looking back, she said thoughtfully, "It's a good thing there's a body outside."

"Why?"

"Vultures."

Lorrie was glad to find Ink in his newspaper office. She'd gone there while Dennis went to buy salve for Pewter's wound. "You said something about Mrs. Collins looking for her son," she told him without preamble. "I thought of her when we went by the old boarding house. We were careful to avoid it, as you suggested, but I looked off in that direction, thinking of her and curious, and I saw vultures over where it might be. I'm just guessing, but I thought maybe someone ought to check. Maybe they've killed someone."

"And you're telling me and not the sheriff. Why not?"

"Because of what you said about him. You're a newspaper man, and I thought you might be interested and might take some men for witnesses." She paused. "It's probably too early for a hearse. After all, it could be a deer or a cow."

He sat down in his office chair and leaned back. "You going to join us?"

"Heavens no. I've got a long way to go to find a pack train and supplies. I can wait and read about it in your paper—if there's anything to tell." She wasn't certain if she should smile or not, so she didn't.

"Want me to send you a copy? Give me your address."

She shook her head. "We don't have addresses yet. Maybe I'll stop by another time. Save me one if you would." Then Dennis was at the door, and she used that as an excuse to say good-bye. She stopped at the door to add, "Don't waste time. You can't tell with vultures—of any sort." She tried to give him a meaningful glance and hoped she succeeded.

The rest of their trip to the muleskinner's ranch was quiet, and there was already a pack train heading out, but there were a number of mules in the corral. Lorrie watched the mules as they went by, studying the packs and trying to estimate how much was in a load. Some of the packs were fairly bulky she noticed. Then she joined Dennis at the corral. He was talking to a man sitting on the fence.

Dennis introduced them when she arrived. "Lorrie, this is Moses Easton. Mr. Easton, this is Miss Lorena Emerson, my aunt. As I said, we need supplies for our settlement further west."

The man jumped down from the fence to shake Lorrie's hand after carefully wiping it on his overalls. "Call me Jack," he told her. "It's short for Jackass. Someone thought it was funny, and it stuck." He shrugged. "Now I don't mind it. I'm even sorry I knocked him down. How big a train do you need?"

"You only have seven mules here, and I don't think that's enough. I want to get all the supplies I can while I'm here."

"There are a few more out in the pasture. You have the supplies brought here, and I'll decide how many you need. Oh, you'll be paying for the guards too. Some Injuns are getting restless, I hear."

"How many do you need? We can help out."

"Nope. I don't go out without my own men" He shook his head firmly. "Now I'll get you a list of places where you can get good prices on grub and other supplies. Have everything sent here. They're used to working with me. When you're done, I decide what and where to pack it and when we leave. You can trail along or go ahead. Up to you," and he headed for the ranch house.

Lorrie frowned after him, and Dennis laughed. "You can't expect him to let you guard the mule train."

Lorrie turned her frown on him, and he laughed again. "Tell you what, you and Jake can go ahead and watch for ambushes." She perked up at that, and Dennis relaxed. A quiet trip would be a nice change, and if anyone attacked the train, they'd deserve what they got.

Lorrie was glad to find everything on the lists Elizabeth, Hannah, and Carrol had given her. George was still hoping for a puppy—he'd given her a list too—but his mother said that a cat was what they needed to keep the mice down in the store. However, she winked at Lorrie, which she took as encouragement to keep her eyes open for a pup. Naturally, the lists included what the men wanted too.

There were only six outriders and eleven mules when they left; and the man in charge of their train was a youngster, Lorrie thought, but he'd teethed on a pack, he told them. "And Jackass is my grandfather. Dad's out with another pack train. We supply the forts and trading posts up the trail, and they supply the wagon trains and whoever comes by."

Lorrie had thought that eleven mules weren't enough for all she'd bought, but the men kept on packing them until everything was loaded. Jack had asked if he could use Jake, but she said only that she used him for riding sometimes. He'd exclaimed when Jake wandered off during the loading, but didn't pursue the matter when Lorrie ignored it.

He hung around until Jake came back and nodded, satisfied. "I see you've got a good one," he told her. "Reminds me of Old Satan. Hell on wheels, but a good 'un to have in a tight spot."

"I hope you weren't too disappointed at the trip home," Dennis said softly when they pulled up in front of the Johnson's store, "but sometimes you can give others a chance."

"All those guards probably scared people away," she retorted in a disappointed tone. And she laughed at his startled look. He laughed then, too, as he realized she actually was joking, but he was still relieved it had been a quiet trip because his main worry had been that he'd disappoint her.

Elizabeth had sent two of her sons out to alert the others that the train had arrived, and they began arriving before it was all unloaded. Carrol loaded Lorrie's small wagon with the goods that belonged to her and Hannah, while Elizabeth's children and her husband carried their supplies into the store. Cupboards, bins, and crocks were waiting to receive the precious cargo.

Of course, the first items distributed were the livestock: three cows due to freshen; a small flock of chickens carried in three crates, each perched on its own mule; and a coonhound puppy for George, along with a gray tabby for his mother and a ginger tabby for Carrol. Lorrie looked over the scene with satisfaction, before plunging into the chaos to separate the bacon, sausage, and cheese she'd marked out for herself. She made sure they went into her space; she wasn't going to clutter up the Michaels' cabin.

After the mules and escorts had left and nothing was left sitting out, Lorrie relaxed in one of the rockers on the store's front porch; it was one of two rockers there. Both had always belonged to the Johnson's. Lorrie's rocking chair, picked up along the trail, was behind the growing collection of her belongings stored in a corner downstairs. George played out front in the dirt with his new puppy.

Elizabeth came out of the store and sat herself down in the adjoining rocker. "It rejoices my heart to see the store so full. You got everything I asked for, and before long I hope to be making butter. Oh, I've missed butter."

Lorrie. "Me too. I look forward to toast and hotcakes. And I hope I got enough flour to make doughnuts some day."

"I'll put that on the list of things I owe you, girl. We'll be paying you back for a long time."

"As long as it includes meals, I'm happy,"

"I know your purse must be getting low."

"I am haggling more than I used to," Lorrie admitted. She was sure she had enough for more necessities, but her money belt was a lot thinner than it used to be. Hoping to change the subject, she leaned forward and called to George, "Have you named your pup yet, George?"

He stood up, holding the puppy in his arms as it happily licked his face. "I've named her Sugar 'cause she's so sweet," he said proudly.

His mother laughed. "Now you can teach her not to chase the chickens," she reminded him.

"She'd never do that!"

"She'd better not," Elizabeth said sternly, and sat back. "Are you going to stick around for a while, now that you've gotten everything, Lorrie? With all the seed you brought, we can finish the planting and start on your cabin."

"The thing is, I didn't get everything we wanted. We need more people—and not just to buy things in your store. We need more skilled people—a blacksmith, miller, schoolteacher, and that's just for starters—and also more young people, so I'm planning to go to some towns and take my time searching for likely folk to meet those needs. The more inhabitants we have, the more who'll come, which also means more security. And we need a name, so people will know where to come when we say home."

"You just don't stop planning, do you, girl? Well, I'm going back inside to see how Sallie Sue's coming with her accounts. Then I'll start on supper. Why don't you join us here, tonight. I know you don't want to make a nuisance of yourself, but I owe you years of meals, probably. In the meantime, why not see if you can get the others to come here tomorrow for a town meeting. I know right now, they're busy unpacking and stowing. We need to make plans before you start out."

The next morning after breakfast—Lorrie had hers with Carrol and Dennis because she'd stay there until she had her own cabin—the valley's and hills' inhabitants gathered on and around the Johnson's General Store front porch. Lorrie had invited the Summers family too, and even Many Stars was there, though she stayed close to her husband. After admiring the store's new sign, everyone looked up at Elizabeth and Lorrie who stood at the porch railing.

After politely waiting for the other to speak, Lorrie stepped back so Elizabeth took the lead. She pointed to Lorrie and said, "She'll be off again soon, prospecting for townsfolk this time. We can't expect her to coax anyone to come to a place that doesn't have a name. We should have a mayor and other officials, too, so none of the newcomers try to take over what we built." She paused as the crowd nodded and agreed. Most of them had been too busy to think about that.

George stood up and announced. "How about Sugar Valley?"

His mother laughed. "It sure does sound like a sweet name, Georgie, but we have to give the others a chance to share their choices."

"Golden Valley. Twilight Valley. River's Bend…." There was a variety of tentative offerings.

"How about Sarah's Valley," Roland, the Johnson's oldest, chimed in. "'Cause that's why we stopped here."

"I like your choice, son," Samuel Johnson told him, "but I think we should avoid anyone's names."

Roland sat down, disappointed.

"We don't want names that you find in every state and territory," Dennis said thoughtfully. After a lot of discussion, the only name they could agree on was Sugar Valley. "A town named after a dog?!" "You have to admit, a town named after a dog isn't something you'll find in every state and territory."

After that, they elected Samuel Johnson mayor despite his protests, "I don't want to be mayor; I don't have the time!"

"Lizzy can help you, Sam," Lorrie reassured him. "And I think Sallie Sue or Carrol will have to be the schoolteacher 'til we find another one. I need to be able to tell people that we have a name, a mayor, a schoolteacher—all the things they're used to in a town. And stake any claims you're thinking about in town while I'm gone, but especially, don't forget my cabin!"

After everyone promised that her cabin would be their next project—after the plowing, the planting, the well digging, and the garden weeding, they went home. She knew they were joking; hopefully she'd have a cabin by the end of the summer.

The next morning, she harnessed Shadow and Sunny to the small wagon and put Jake's saddle and pack in it, along with Shadow's. She planned to bring back things that hadn't been on the supplies list, including plants for the garden, fruit trees, and flowers. She'd had breakfast with the Johnson's; Elizabeth encouraged her to eat there often to make a dent in the debt they owed her.

Chapter Ten
~ Prospecting for Settlers ~

Lorrie had hoped to take Starlight with her this trip, but she couldn't go. "When I told Mother about being called half breed at the fort, she wouldn't let me go back there or anywhere, it looks like."

"Did you tell your father, too?" Star nodded. "Oh, I bet he was mad as hell." Star nodded again.

Lorrie didn't want to take Dennis 'cause that would slow her cabin down, among other chores that needed to be done, and Carrol was torn between wanting to go and finishing her garden and helping with other projects. They both decided it was best for her to stay.

Once on the trail, Lorrie relished her freedom, though. It reminded her of the beginning of her solo journey. She liked the challenges, as well as the people she met along the way. She spent her time on the wagon seat making plans and thinking about the future. She knew, from talking to Carrol, that she wanted to find a husband and make a home. Lorrie searched her thoughts and decided that she liked being free. She watched Jake running alongside the wagon, when he wasn't behind or ahead of it. He obviously appreciated not being harnessed to a wagon.

She decided not to go back to the towns she knew. She had never explored Rocky Falls. She didn't even know how big it was, and it would be interesting to find out what had happened there, after she and Dennis left. She'd be cautious though and see how Ink behaved, before venturing into town. She was grateful that Territory Tales was on the edge of town.

She left the wagon behind the building and didn't unharness the horses in case she was in a hurry to leave. She went in the back door; the press wasn't running so the building didn't shake, and she could look through the rooms quietly. She found Ink leaning back in his office chair reading a newspaper and marking the pages with a pencil and muttering.

"Too many typos?" she asked.

He lowered the paper, and looked up at her and smiled. "I have an apprentice who makes up his own words," he informed her. "I have your paper in a drawer here," he told her. "More than one in fact. The town got pretty excited. You'll enjoy the story where the sheriff was chased out of town and a new one elected. No proof that he was involved, or they'd have hung him," he added soberly.

"What did they find? I'll take the papers—and pay you, of course."

"No need. I owe you for the scoop. Well, I talked to some people I knew would be interested, including Mrs. Collins and her family, which is quite a clan, by the way, saying only that someone had reported vultures at the old trail stop and that something might have happened there that needed to be investigated. That person told me because it was news and because maybe the sheriff couldn't be trusted. I said I was going right out there, to see if there was a story, and that company would be nice, in case of any trouble."

He stopped to see if she was paying attention. She was, and he couldn't help smiling; he was a newspaperman because he loved a good story. "Mrs. Collins gathered the men in her clan, others came, too, out of curiosity, and later the undertaker showed up there with his hearse. You didn't tell him, did you?" She shook her head violently. "You'll be surprised to learn, then," he said, studying her face, "that there was a body in the front yard, and three more upstairs, also dead. The men scattered, searching the house and barn, and a couple called out from the barn that they'd found something there. What do you think it was?"

Lorrie looked at him. "I am waiting impatiently—very impatiently—for you to tell me," she said. "Hurry up!"

He stopped smiling, and looked grimly at the floor. "There were coins and watches on the barn floor, and the men began casting around to see what it meant. Eventually they tore the barn apart, and that's when they found the pit under the floorboards in a stall. It was full of a pitiful amount of remains and quicklime. Scattered elsewhere under the floors in the house, which they began ripping apart after the discovery in the barn, they found more watches, money, belts, and things that might catch a magpie's fancy. Among these things were Mrs. Collins' son's pocket watch and a locket with his girlfriend's hair in it. They were all sorry that there was no one left to kill. You'll be interested to know, that all those horses and men and the hearse erased any sign of who had done it. They're guessing that the men ran into someone they couldn't handle. Stupid of them, after all these years."

Lorrie sat down in another chair that he offered her, then. She hadn't spent much time thinking about the victims. She swallowed. "I'm glad they found all that. It needed to be found."

"It was certainly time for it," he agreed. "Thank you." When she looked at him questioningly, he said, "For telling me about the vultures." She nodded.

After leaving Ink's office, she drove the wagon to the hotel and registered for a room and arranged for Jake and the horses to be stabled. She told Jake to stay and not come looking for her, which puzzled the hostler; he was even more confused when she said, "If he gets out, don't worry about it. He thinks he's a dog. Just leave him alone." the hostler nodded, but shook his head after she left. He and Jake stared at each other, until he left to get back to mucking out stalls.

Lorrie's first stop was at the town's general store. She could compare it to their own and see if it had anything she could use. As she browsed the fabric selection, a loud voice suddenly interrupted the quiet of the room. "You stupid girl. I told you to put the shirts on the top shelf and the trousers on the middle shelf. Now do it over, and this time get it right." Then she returned to a back room, from which she had apparently emerged.

When Lorrie turned to look, thinking—sounds like a bully to me—she saw that the stupid girl was actually a young woman—and not so young. She stared up at the top shelf and went to pull a stool from under the front counter. Observing her, Lorrie noticed the candy selection on top of the counter and determined to buy most of that before she left.

Giving a quick glance behind her to be sure they were still alone, she crossed over to where the woman had climbed up on the stool and was pulling the shirts down, teeth still clenched. "Hand them down to me," Lorrie told her. "It'll save you climbing up and down. Tough boss, huh." she added.

The woman looked at her. "My mother-in-law."

Lorrie's eyes widened. "Where's your husband?" Maybe he's dead, she thought.

"Delivering supplies to one of the outlying ranches."

"So, did you really get the shelves wrong?"

"No. She likes to do that. I think she hopes I'll fall and break my neck."

Lorrie hissed, and the woman looked at her in alarm. Must not do that, Lorrie told herself for the umpteenth time. "Where does your husband stand in all this?"

The woman sighed, and her eyes softened. "Not his fault. He just can't stand up to her. His brother escaped, with the help of his wife. I'm not strong enough, maybe. I don't know what to do."

Just then, the woman erupted out of the back room again. "Don't just stand there. Get back to work," she commanded.

Lorrie turned and moved a few steps closer. "She's helping me with my choices. Go away until I need your help." She smiled with a show of teeth, and the older woman retreated into the back room, muttering something about uppity women.

"I could never do that. I think she'd hit me." And flushing, she looked away.

"You don't have to take that approach, of course," Lorrie reassured her. "And by the by, what is your name? I'm Lorrie Emerson.

"I'm Catherine Carruthers. You can call me Cathy. SHE calls me stupid girl and sometimes slut, but she doesn't say that in front of Fred. She never thought I was good enough for her boy."

"Hmm. Have you ever thought of leaving?"

Cathy was shocked. "Never. I would never leave Frederick. It's hard living in the same house and never being able to get away from her, but he's there too," she said simply. "And we save money by living in her big house, and he's there to help if she needs help."

"Actually, I was thinking more of leaving the house—and the town and starting a new life." Cathy shook her head until her blonde hair tumbled down around her face. "If he loves you, even half as much as you love him, I think he might come after you. 'Course I can't promise you that's how it'll work out, but you can always go back."

"I don't know if I'd want to go back—maybe. You see, here the whole town knows my family." She was staring at a shelf full of trousers and was at least considering the idea, Lorrie thought. "Where would I go? What would I do?"

"Making a new life is never easy, but I know a town that needs settlers. You could maybe start a hotel." Lorrie was scrabbling for ideas. "Not a big hotel, but with maybe a little restaurant or café. Can you cook? Do you have furniture and linens? Any money?"

"I can cook. At least I used to. She says I'm not good enough, and she does all the cooking. I can do dishes, though," she said with a half smile. And I've got my hope chest because my things weren't good enough for her house or her boy. What's the name of the town?"

"Sugar Valley," Lorrie said, smiling in remembrance.

"What a pretty name! Is there a building for a hotel?" Cathy was thinking now and almost ready to make the jump.

Lorrie sighed. "No building. All the buildings are taken, but there are men to help build, and I could lend you the money for the building and what you need, and you could pay me back. I have to say," and Lorrie looked her straight in the eye, "that there wouldn't be a lot of business right away; you might have to work besides."

And I might have to work, too, at the rate I'm spending money, Lorrie thought. 'Course I am owed a lot, and I shouldn't run out of food—or at least meals—for years. But she smiled cheerfully and said. "Your decision. I'll be in town for another day or two, and I've got room in my wagon for your things—at the moment. You can find me at the hotel. Now you'd better put the shirts where they belong."

Lorrie's next stop was at the blacksmith's. A small, but brawny man was working at the anvil with a hot piece of iron while a younger, taller man was pumping the bellows. Lorrie waited until the man had put the iron rod aside to see what she wanted. "I'm looking for a blacksmith for the settlement," she told him.

"Much business there?"

"Not much," she admitted, "but you could pick you own site, and it's a growing community."

"I've got plenty of business here. And my family's here. And I sure don't want to move this anvil again." It certainly was big, but Lorrie had no idea how big they got.

"I've got an anvil," the younger man said, glancing sidewise at the blacksmith. "It's smaller, and the point's broken off, but I've got a few hammers too, and I've been an apprentice for a long time. And you know that Christopher would love the chance to take over for me." Now he looked straight at the blacksmith. Then he waited, so Lorrie waited too.

The blacksmith looked at Lorrie instead. "He's good. 'Course he hasn't learned all he could, but some of that he'll learn hisself. I think you couldn't find a better choice. Not around here at any rate, since I'm not in the race," and he winked at her before turning to the other man. "Go show 'em what I learned you, Tucker. Make me proud. And come visit me and your ma some times." He turned to Lorrie, "Tell me who I'm entrusting my boy to. I'm Torrance Bradley, and he's Tucker." Then he clapped his son on the back. "Get your tools, boy."

Things were moving right along finally, Lorrie thought. "I'm Lorena Emerson, and I've got a wagon at the hotel," she told them. She left the son packing his anvil and tools, and she hoped, clothes, though obviously tools came first. Lorrie spent the rest of the day and the next working her way through the town, planting seeds with visions of opportunity. "You'll be among the first," she said more than once, "and you'll have your choice of prime land. And we have a schoolteacher." Oops, better add a school to the list of buildings they were going to need.

The third day, Lorrie was packing things she'd bought, including candy, bread, cheese, and even butter. She planned to use it up on the trail before it went rancid. Everything went neatly around the anvil, tools, and Tucker's pack. She'd given up looking for Cathy, which would give her more room for last minute purchases. Yes, she'd go get those fruit trees now. They were small enough to tuck in amongst the barrels, and she had made sure the water barrels along the wagon bed were full.

"Miss Emerson, please wait!" It was Catherine with a note of desperation in her tone. "Have you saved room for my chest and my clothes?" She was carrying a birdcage, along with a large suitcase, and there was a coat draped around her shoulders.

"Of course, Cathy." But it was a good thing she'd had plenty of practice packing wagons and mules because some things Jake would have to carry. "My chest and other things are on the porch back at the house. Can you bring the wagon, please?" Cathy was almost crying.

Lorrie hoped she wasn't responsible for breaking up a home, unhappy though it was. You are responsible, she admitted to herself. Don't make excuses. "What happened?"

"Fred was in the barn, and she bumped me in the kitchen, and I broke a dish, and she said I was lazy and good-for-nothing and she felt sorry for her son, being stuck with me because he was too good-hearted to kick me out. She said she was just sorry that she couldn't do it. I stepped close to her, and I was angry, she could tell because I never went close to her unless I had to, and I felt like I was on fire, and then I…"

Lorrie was holding her breath, and Tucker was listening too. He'd stayed back at first, but now he was as anxious to hear what happened as Lorrie was. "What happened?!" Lorrie practically cried out.

"I looked at her and smiled, because it felt so good making up my mind, and I said good-bye, and went upstairs to pack. Fred came in as I was trying to get my chest down the stairs. He'd come through the kitchen, and his face was pale. I don't know what she told him, and I didn't care. I didn't say anything, but thank you when he put my things on the porch. I didn't say good-bye to him. I couldn't. I hope he thinks about what that means." She stopped out of breath because she was still panting.

"So, we're going to your house now to pick up your things," Lorrie asked. She wanted to be sure.

"Not my house. Her house. I'm going to have my own house. Aren't we, Fife," she said, bending down to speak into the birdcage. Fife was a canary. And so the four of them went to the Carruthers house, and Frederick Carruthers silently piled everything Catherine Carruthers owned in the wagon. Lorrie lost no time heading out of town. She'd repack on the trail and hope nothing fell off before then.

To make conversation, Lorrie asked what the hotel's name meant when they passed it. "What does The Robin's Nest mean?" She was instantly sorry she'd mentioned a hotel.

Cathy merely glanced at it, however. "The owner named it after his little girl, Robin. She's grown now and married. I'll have to think of a name for my hotel, won't I?"

She was quiet for a while, and Tucker asked, "Where are we going? I was too excited to ask you before. Is it far?"

"We're going to Sugar Valley," Cathy told him. "It's really pretty, isn't it, Lorrie?"

"Yes, very," was all Lorrie said as she pulled off the road to repack the wagon; Tucker helped her, and Jake didn't have to carry as much as she feared. They made a snug hole for Fife's cage to keep it steady. Climbing back on the wagon seat and clucking to Sunny and Shadow to move on, she thought about the question a little more.

"There's our valley with another one nearby, though that floods. We use it for pasture mostly; and then there's the mountains off to the west, of course. We're in the foothills, though they can be really steep. You'll want to be in the valley or in the town, which we're still building. You can choose your sites. Tucker, you'll want a house somewhere separate from the smithy, but you can live in the hotel, Cathy. As long as you want to. You both know that you'll have to build, but we'll help you, and we've got the rest of the summer." She hoped her cabin was done because she was now responsible for their habitations.

The wagon was full, and Jake had to be unpacked and packed each night and morning so it took a few days longer to get home, but at last Lorrie pulled up in front of the Johnson's General Store. She thought Sam's sign made it look like a real store. Clifford, the Johnson's middle boy, was the first to spot her. He came running around the house to greet her and the newcomers.

"Ma, Ma, they're here," he yelled. Then he perched on the porch railing to give her the news. "Your house is almost done, Miss Lorrie; it would have been done sooner, but Evan hurt his leg when the wagon tipped, and he had to jump clear of the logs. But he's been working on the shingles after that so we have lots."

Elizabeth Johnson was wiping her hands on her apron when she came out on the porch. "I had to finish putting the pies in the oven, or I'd been out straightaway. I suppose Cliff has told you that your house is almost done. Brock came down to help after Evan twisted his leg. The wagon lost a wheel when it went over, but Evan used the wheel from his old wagon. He was happy about that, though he's still grumbling about being so clumsy he hurt himself. The slope was just too steep, and the wagon slid and then fell over. The horses weren't hurt, thank the Lord, so we're in fine shape. Now let's get to the introductions. I'm Elizabeth Johnson, and this is Clifford, who's been out back weeding the garden."

Cliff looked at his mother to see if she was going to send him right back, but she didn't. She smiled at him and let him stay, so he relaxed and focused on the newcomers.

Lorrie was going to let them introduce themselves, but they looked at her, so she began. "This is Catherine Carruthers; she's going to build her hotel here. And Tucker's our new blacksmith. He needs a place for his smithy and his home."

Elizabeth frowned a little. "You can't put it where the runoff goes into the river or the town," she said firmly.

"No, ma'am. My father taught me how to avoid any problems like that. Can I look around to find the right site?"

"Good idea, young man. Go ahead, but maybe you'd like to settle in and eat first. I certainly want you to stick around for some apple pie. You can wash up out back. You too, miss."

Neither Lorrie or Cathy corrected her, and when the two had gone around back, Elizabeth asked, "Where are we going to put them up?"

"She can stay with me because I'm not expecting you to put them up," Lorrie hastened to assure her. "Tucker could stay with Dennis if Carrol stayed with me too. Or else…"

"Hmm. She have any money for building that hotel?"

"Nope, I'll help with that."

"How about if she stayed here and took care of little Sarah while I go help with the gardens or building. I'd be so happy to get out for a while.'

"Excellent plan, Lizzy. Then you can pay her, which will probably make her feel better too."

"I'll get inside and check on those pies. You bring them on in. You can unpack later."

"I'll be in as soon as I unpack Jake," Lorrie promised.

Chapter Eleven
~ They Will Come ~

Cathy Carruthers and Tucker Bradley were the first. In less than a month Frederick Carruthers arrived with a wagonload of furniture and supplies. The hotel had a partial basement; Cathy had decided to start small with a four room cabin on the back of the property and build on in front when she could pay for it by herself. Her husband admired her work and her plans, and before he had decided how to approach her about staying there, she had him planning where to put the livery stable and starting a well uphill from the buildings. After that, they added a porch, and onlookers could hear him whistling while laying floorboards and pounding nails.

"I didn't see much of him there," Lorrie told Lizzie, "but he seems a lot happier here.

Elizabeth nodded. "While you were up fixing up your place, his brother came and begged him to come back for his mother's sake. Fred said, 'I wouldn't come back from hell for her,' and he meant it."

In a few more months, two families arrived. They had heard about Sugar Valley and left their wagon train. Over the next year a few more trickled in, and a mason started work on the Johnson's brick house the following summer; he made the bricks himself downstream with a clay deposit he'd found after looking around for a week. Lorrie had found him at Fort Laramie working on new buildings there.

She also arranged to have lumber poled up from down the river, but she no longer had to pay for building and supplies as the other settlers took on that responsibility themselves; and she continued to draw on her credit at the store and meals there and elsewhere. Hannah told her once, “Evan and I owe you for the rest of our lives. Don’t you forget it, ’cause we sure don’t intend to.”

So it was, that one late spring morning two years later, she sat on her front porch eating an early lunch of fresh-baked bread from Carrol, along with sausage and cheese. She’d finished the milk at supper—before it turned. She’d get some again tonight, when Dennis milked. She’d pulled a butter churn from the furniture at the general store. It’d give her something to do until she decided where to go next. Staying put was not something she could do for very long.

And then she saw a shadow slinking along the side of the porch, and the next instant there was a wolf standing almost on top of her. It sniffed the bread, which she immediately held out to him, but he ignored it and stared into her face. Shadow was in the valley grazing, and Sunny was in the corral for when Lorrie needed her. Sunny snorted and then whickered uneasily. Then they both heard the thundering of hooves, and Jake burst out of the woods above the cabin and headed for them at a full gallop.

The wolf considered the situation, leapt off the porch, and circled around the cabin with Jake in hot pursuit. They circled the cabin three times before the wolf fled into the woods. Jake started after him, but Lorrie called him back. “You know, Jake,” she said to the mule, who’d taken up guard duty near the porch, “I think he just got tired of playing. I don’t think he’s rabid or hungry, but I think I’ll save him some bread and meat just in case.”

Lorrie couldn’t make up her mind whether to retreat into the cabin or make a run for it to town. Town, our own town, she mused, distracted by the thought for a bit, but before she could get up and go inside, the wolf was back, carrying something in his teeth. Jake lowered his head, laid his ears back, and pawed the ground, but the wolf sat quiet and watchful, letting Jake approach him. They almost touched noses, but instead, Jake sniffed the rag the wolf was carrying, then led the way to the porch.

When the wolf leaped onto the porch again, Jake leapt up after him, startling the wolf that went belly down and snarled before he realized that the mule was merely watching. The wolf then dropped the bloody rag in Lorrie’s lap. Yes, it was certainly a bloody rag. A piece of shirt, perhaps. When she didn’t move, the wolf nudged her arm, and Jake’s ears went forward, and he bared his teeth.

"It's all right, Jake. He's telling me I need to hurry. Tell him I have to saddle you and get a few things." The wolf waited impatiently, but as soon as Lorrie mounted Jake and headed towards the wolf, it was off. The trio went farther up the mountain, waded a creek, and shoved into the brush growing along the bank.

They shoved their way further in through some brambles—raspberries that she made a note of, for future harvesting—and then she saw the body. "Good hiding place," she remarked, as she pulled off her saddle bag and canteen and was enveloped in thorns. She'd been pretty sure the wolf would know if the man was dead, so she turned the man over and poured some water into his mouth to see if he could swallow. At first he didn't, but the wolf pawed his shoulder, and he took a few sips.

She succeeded in turning him over more, so she could find the wound. Oh, oh. Two arrows. One in his shoulder and one—no two—in his right leg; and there was a gash in his lower right arm. Knife or hatchet. Not a good sign. At least she had Jake and a wolf to protect her. She gave Jake the down command, and he knelt next to the man. With her shoving and the wolf pulling, they stretched him over the saddle. She got on and held him tight, and Jake rose to his feet and headed back down the mountain.

At first she thought of taking him to the Browns' cabin because it was closer, but she changed her mind when she realized that the Summers would be better able to deal with the problem. Many Stars had doubtless patched her husband up more than once, and Brock would know what to do about the Indians. The wolf trailed along behind, keeping watch on his master, she thought, but when he vanished into the woods periodically, she thought that he might be watching for Indians. She felt a little safer.

At the Summers', she rode Jake up to the porch and slid off onto it, so she could catch the man when she pulled him off, and she called into the open door—Brock, Star. I need help out here. Many Stars was there first, followed by Starlight. Between the three of them, they half-carried and half-dragged him into the cabin and onto a big bed in the back room.

"Where's your father?" Lorrie asked Star, as she panted and caught her breath. That man was heavy!

"He's up a ways. He's checking the near traps today so I can bring him back right away," but when she reached for the rifle on the wall, her mother stopped her and grabbed it herself, giving her a sharp command. "I can't go because it's not safe," Star told Lorrie. She wasn't happy, but she obeyed.

The two girls washed the blood off his arm, face, and beard. Star held him up while Lorrie did that so that the arrow wouldn't be driven farther into his back. "Mother always pulled the arrows out. I don't want to hurt him, and the wounds aren't bleeding as much. I think we should leave them."

Lorrie nodded. She didn't want to be the one who did that, but she'd better watch so she could. It was probably a couple hours before they heard the thudding hoof beats of running horses. Brock burst into the cabin and looked at the wounded man. "Send your mother in, Star, and you put the horses in the barn. Come right back after you see if it's safe," he instructed.

"We've given him some water, and he mostly drinks it," Lorrie told him; then she moved aside when Many Stars came in. The couple cut out the arrows with a knife sterilized with what was probably whiskey, Lorrie guessed.

"The wolf his?"

Lorrie half smiled. "I wouldn't be surprised," she said.

Brock smiled, too, and looked back at the arrows he was holding. "Out of their territory," he said, frowning. "I'll have to backtrack them. You stay put. Jake'll stand watch, and probably the wolf, too." Before he left, he put a knife and hatchet in the front of his belt and another knife behind his back. Many Stars brought another rifle out of the backroom and handed it to him. He took it, then shook his head and handed it back. His wife glared at him, and he kissed the top of her head and laughed. "I'll take a fresh horse. Can't say when I'll be back. You stay, Lorrie, till then. No running off."

"Shouldn't I warn the other cabins?"

He shook his head. "Wait," he repeated. "I'll know more of the lay of the land then."

"What if you don't come back?" Star demanded.

"Avenge me," he said, "after warning the others." Many Stars gave him a sack of bread and jerky before he left. Then she sat in the cabin door and shelled corn while keeping an eye on Jake in the front of the cabin and the horses in the corral for signs of alarm.

At dark, they all went inside, but not until Many Stars brought in buckets of water to fill the water barrel; then she set the full water buckets next to it. Star kept watch in the doorway with the rifle, 'til her mother was safe inside. Then she bolted the door.

It was late morning the next day, when Brock returned. They all went down to the corral to meet him as he unsaddled and rubbed down his horse. Many Stars questioned him in her language while he worked. "Not to worry," he said, rubbing the horse down with firm strokes. "I found two dead Indians and three others. Two were wounded. The man is a good fighter. 'Course, most of them had bite marks and torn clothing. Good thing he had that wolf."

"Where are they now?" Lorrie asked. She wanted to be sure.

"Dead. I dumped the bodies down a gulley. I think he had a horse once. There was a saddle pack further back. I put it in the barn with my horse's saddle. How's he doing?"

Lorrie looked at Many Stars. "Better," she told him. "Lost much blood. I will give him soup. It cooking now."

Brock soon sent Lorrie home. "We don't need you to feed him, too. You go and warn the others, but tell them no need to panic. Of course, it always pays to be alert, and I'm going to scout in a bigger circle now. I needed to give you the news, or I'd still be out there."

"Be careful," she told him, loathe to leave the man she had rescued. Later she saddled Jake and headed to the Brown's before going on to the Michael's and the town. The wolf watched her to the edge of the clearing before going back in the cabin.

Brock came home in a few days. "No other sign," he told Lorrie, who was at the cabin again. She was there almost every day to check on progress, so she was there when the stranger came to for the first time, and when Brock shaved him. That brush pile had hidden a handsome face, she thought. He certainly looked like the mountain men who visited the Summers' cabin now and then. After that, she grew shy and spent her time catching up with the weeds in her garden and helping Hannah milk and do other chores, so Hannah could spend her time baking bread and cooking enough chicken and venison stew to share with the Summers, since they had another mouth to feed.

Lorrie was sweeping the cabin floor at last, after being busy helping Cathy Carruthers put up curtains in the hotel addition in the valley. She came out when she heard the sound of Jake's hooves nearing the cabin and stopped at the door within reach of her favorite rifle; then she saw the man coming down the path from the Summers'. She would have known him even without the gray wolf at his side. He was pale and thinner than when she'd first seen him, but he walked easily. She knew he'd had to hang on to the furniture when he first got up. Star had told her.

He stopped at the bottom of the porch steps, but the wolf came on up. "I've come to thank you. They told me you saved my life."

"You owe a lot to your wolf also," she said. "What's his name? I've often wondered."

"Gray Cloud." He looked down at the wolf. "Good Cloud," he said softly. "Good boy." He looked back at her, "and I'm Barrett Lee."

"Lorena Emerson," she said holding out her hand. He came up the steps to take it. They both knew each other's names actually—but only second hand. However, it was the polite thing to do and enabled them to start a conversation.

"Mind if I set a spell," he asked. "That's a steep trail." She saw that it had tired him out more than he'd ever admit to.

"I'll get you some water to drink—and perhaps an early supper." She looked at the sun; it was a ways from setting, but he did need to build up his strength. She'd been going to go to the Michaels' for supper and to help Carrol with the dishes, but she could do that any time, so she made toast over the open fire in the fireplace, got butter where it was sitting in the bucket in the cool water in the well, and even fried some bacon and potatoes.

They ate companionably on the porch, and he shifted his leg every so often. It'd be a while before he could go back to his trail, she thought. He left well before dark, so he could find his way, and after that, he came down every day. He needed to exercise his leg, he told her. One day after he'd gone back to the Summers', she rode Jake down to the general store with a pack and stocked up on food. "Something that's easy to cook would be nice," she told Sallie Sue.

Sallie Sue's mouth twitched. "When did you start cooking?" she teased.

"Oh, I get company now and then," Lorrie answered. She knew everyone knew about the stranger and his visits. The Johnson children had even taken to coming by so they could see the wolf.

Further into summer, Barrett's leg was stronger, and he began running down the path and up again. Exercising it, she realized. He also seemed less content during his visits and looked up at the mountain now and then. One day he asked, “Is there anything I can do for you? I’m beholden to you; I can help with wood cutting. I see you don’t have any wood yet, for the coming winter.”

He looked at the cabin door, and she coaxed him in, with an offer of cornbread. He studied the fireplace. “That uses a lot of wood. You don’t have a woodstove, I see.”

“Nope.” She didn’t tell him that she’d ordered one and it was its way. She also didn’t tell him that she was going to pick it up soon. He’d volunteer for that. He could help her and get out of the cabins that were possibly beginning to stifle him. Brock had told her something about mountain men. As a matter of fact, he’d mentioned it more often lately.

And that reminded her of a conversation a couple women had had in a general store a while back while she was there picking up more potatoes, salt, and some candy. “It’s not always easy getting a man to come up to scratch,” the older woman told the younger one. “It’s a lot easier scaring them off by getting romantic and possessive.” It sounded to Lorrie as if she spoke from personal experience.

Lorrie began her attack on the porch as they sat munching cornbread. She touched his arm and batted her eyes. “It’s so nice having a man around the cabin,” she said. “You sure make a woman feel safe.” She batted her eyes again and hoped she wouldn’t puke. Or maybe he would. “You should come down for breakfast some morning. Real early.” This time she didn’t bat her eyes. She pressed his arm instead.

She wasn’t surprised when he slid away, stood up, and mumbled something about getting back to help Brock milk the horses or something. Men, she thought, in relief and maybe a hint of regret. She wasn’t surprised when Brock came down the next afternoon and told her that their visitor had gone. Brock had taken him to town to buy a horse and was now on his way home. “What did you say to him, girl?” he demanded.

She shook her head and grinned. “Men are so predictable,” was all she’d say.

Chapter Twelve
~ On the Trail Again ~

Before the week's end, Lorrie, Rollie, Dennis, and Carrol Johnson were on the trail to Rocky Falls in the big wagon. Abe and Sarah, the Shires, were pulling it because they were going to pick up the wood stove, and some beds and other furniture for Sugar Valley.

After parking the wagon behind the hotel and arranging to stable the horses, they stopped at the general store to check on their purchases. "I'm glad you came for them," the store owner said. "A lot of people wanted the beds and chests, but more wanted those mattresses."

Dennis smiled. "Straw-stuffed mattresses aren't real comfortable, even after you've piled them high with blankets. I promised Carrol these last year."

"I've been looking forward to mine for a long time, even more than the stove. I'm used to the fireplace, even though I don't cook all that much." A stove is better, Lorrie, Carrol had promised.

Roland looked at Lorrie, curious. "You really goin' to cook?"

"Hannah said she'd give me a refresher course once I had the stove. I did do some."

Dennis laughed. "Makes me recall how good Hannah's food is." They decided they'd leave the next day and load up the wagon then, so they strolled to the hotel. After registering, Rollie, Carrol and Dennis went to explore the town, and Lorrie walked up to Territory Tales.

She heard the printing press as she approached, but it didn't sound as thunderous as she remembered, so she wasn't surprised to see a new one in the newspaper office; it was also farther back. The building had been expanded, and Ink was sitting at the front desk with two young men sitting at two of the other desks.

He was scribbling busily on a notepad so he didn't see her 'til she bent over to see what he was writing. "Lorrie Emerson! Always a pleasure to see you. Sit here in this chair. I'll move the dictionary first. You here to pick up another load for your settlement? What is the name of it, by the way? Is it on the map yet?" He turned to the two men. "Go out and look for some news. Don't come back until you each have a front page story." He turned back to Lorrie. "That'll keep 'em busy and give us some privacy."

She waited until they were gone to answer his question. "Sugar Valley." It hadn't had a name last time she was here, but she saw no need to mention that. "There are maps of the territory now?"

Ink shrugged. "Bits and pieces anyway. But someone was wondering about what's happening out here. She was curious to know more about everything and everyone."

"Why?" Now Lorrie was curious.

"She was way out here gathering background for a newspaper back in New York City. She wanted to know about the towns, the settlers, the wagon trains, the forts, and the Indians, of course. I let her read back issues of Tales, and she came up to me one day and said, 'What aren't you saying in these stories?'"

"I was surprised and asked her what in the world she meant."

"She had read the story of the robbers and the forgotten hotel and the lime pit. She wanted to know what happened there. I said I couldn't tell her anything because I hadn't been there. No one had been there. She looked annoyed and said flatly that she didn't think I was the ignoramus I pretended to be."

Lorrie laughed. "That's a hard accusation to answer."

Ink nodded. "So I didn't. I told her she should question the sheriff, so she did and she also scoured the town and came back with stuff I didn't know." He gave her a piercing glance, and she braced herself. "Apparently she got a lot of the information from Mrs. Collins. She told this reporter that it was the woman who done it. The one who found her son, led her own wagon train, started a settlement, led a mule train, gathered in settlers like a shepherd, rescued men from Indians, and shot anyone who got in her way."

Lorrie was stunned. "How could she know all that? I'm surprised she didn't mention the wolf and Jake."

"Oh, Lorrie. Those are stories that deserve to be on the front page. I could sell them back east! What's his name?"

"Whose name?" Lorrie swallowed. She'd never been a blabbermouth.

"The wolf's. Jake's your mule, right. The one who thinks he's a dog."

"Good gravy! I said that once, but he doesn't think he's a dog. He knows who he is."

"There's another thing. She wasn't alone. There were two other reporters—men. They split up to cover more territory; and there were two photographers. She had one of them, and he took pictures of buildings and people, and things I never notice anymore." He sighed. "She also told me that my paper was pitiful and boring. Besides real news, it needed pictures, and she gave me some. I used them all, and since the paper was growing—I'm delivering to the forts and towns and even passing settlers now; I added on to the building, bought a new press—well, the press is used, but not as much as my old one—and more help—I bought a camera, and hired a kid who knew how to use it."

Lorrie clasped her hands and bit her lower lip. "You're not going to use all those, uh, stories, are you?"

"Not without a reliable source. You know I never did before," he said reproachfully. "However, she plans to come back and learn more as soon as she can. After she turns in her stories, she's going to come back and write a book."

Lorrie stood up and frowned. She didn't want anyone bothering her or the settlement or even Jake. Ink stood up too. "It's history, Lorrie. It's better to have the truth published than gossip and rumors. I understand that they're writing stories that's already changed what we know to be true, but no one else ever will."

She nodded finally, and she wasn't surprised when he and a photographer were standing by Abe and Sarah, as she came out with another load of material and bed linens for the wagon the next morning

Dennis was brushing Abe, and Carrol was combing Sarah's tail. Dennis looked up, but didn't stop his brushing. "Ink wants to take pictures of Abraham and Sarah and the wagon," he said enthusiastically.

Ink made a few notes on his tablet. "So it's Abraham and not just Abe. We want to get it right." He turned to Lorrie. "I'd like a photograph of Jake, also you and Jake. Just walk up to him and, um, scratch his ears. We don't have to do a full on shot of you, if you don't want. Just a profile. Dennis, will you and Carrol get up on the wagon seat and hold the reins. That'd be good. And can you get up on Jake, Lorrie? Does he have a saddle?"

Lorrie smiled a bit. She was getting into the spirit of things. "Wouldn't it be more exciting without a saddle?"

"You're right, of course. I don't suppose you ever rode side saddle?" he asked curiously.

"Back East. It helped make up my mind to go west."

"Now you're all going to have to hold each pose 'til Toby tells you you can move." Posing for the pictures took up most of the morning, and Lorrie took advantage of the time Toby was spending on the horses and the wagon to ask, "What are you going to do with these photos, Ink?"

"Don't worry. I'm having prints made for you, and I'm saving duplicates for the book if that ever happens. It will be with your permission, of course."

"Thank you." Lorrie was relieved. She needed to know his plans; for now she was safe from the reporter. They ate lunch at the hotel café, and later they drove the wagon to the general store because, while waiting, Lorrie had time to rearrange the wagon and make room for another crock of pickles and a block of cocoa; and Carrol bought a bag of peppermints for the trail.

Later, after handing out more peppermints, Carrol said, "It would have been nice to have pictures of the oxen and the other wagons and the kids. Now everything's changed and they're growing up."

Lorrie considered that for a moment. "Yes, Jemmy and Dolly and the others, but I'd really like to have them in color." A photo of Gray Cloud would have been nice too, she thought.

The trip back was uneventful, and for once, Lorrie found herself looking forward to being home, rather than watching for brigands. She pictured Gray Cloud on her porch—and maybe even Barrett. She and Carrol got to sleep on the new mattresses—they'd packed them that way—while Dennis and Rollie got extra blankets to lie on under the wagon.

Back in Sugar Valley, they unloaded first at the general store, and children were sent out to tell everyone that their orders were in. Lorrie took three pickles out of the crock and made sure that Sallie Sue noted it in her personal ledger. While she did that, little Sarah ran up and wanted to see what was in the crock. Clifford held her up so she could see and smell them. She wrinkled her nose and demanded to be put back on the floor. Elizabeth Johnson brought out rolls fresh from the oven, butter, and baked beans for her to take home with her.

At her cabin, Lorrie sat on the porch and ate the buttered rolls, beans, and a pickle and put the other two in her little crock. After supper she tightened the ropes so the bed would be taut for the new mattress. She'd never had to use a straw mattress, but her old one was thin. She'd put it in the loft for company.

Chapter Thirteen
~ The Prodigal Returns ~

For the first time in almost six years, no one worried about the upcoming winter. Everyone had enough hay, supplies, quilts, and homes. The Johnson's brick home up the valley was finished; the school was finished on the outside. Inside they'd need a wood stove for when school started; Evan was making desks and seats for it. They'd need an outhouse for it later, and it wouldn't be long after that that the girls would be demanding their own. Lorrie's cabin was tightly chinked, but now and then Lorrie could feel the winter winds buffeting the cabin. The snow was thick and deep most of the winter, but the Johnsons had a sleigh and so did the Carruthers. Elizabeth put sleigh bells on her shopping list for next year.

With so much snow, and travel restricted, Lorrie found herself cooking more. She didn't enjoy it the way she knew some women did—cooking for their families, but she thought her corn meal mush, with bacon, was pretty tasty. She was enjoying it one early spring morning on her porch—sitting in the sun kept her warm enough unless there was a cold breeze—when a wolf landed on her porch and sniffed the empty dish.

"Hi, Gray Cloud," she said, in delighted surprise. "I've got some jerky for you 'cause I was only saving it in case I needed it this winter."

"No need," Barrett said. "I killed a deer on the way here. I'll hang it up out back and cut some off to cook." The soft ground had masked the sound of his horse's hooves; now he led the pinto out back; the carcass was slung over the saddle.

Lorrie couldn't think what to say so she simply went into the cabin, put her dish in the dry sink and checked her larder. There were still potatoes, onions, and carrots in the root cellar, and plenty of flour, salt and sugar in the bins. Toasting the old bread and topping it with cheese was always a good idea.

Barrett hesitated in the doorway even as Cloud sniffed his way around the cabin and climbed the ladder to the loft. "Can I come in?" he asked hesitantly. "I can always leave it on the porch if you'd rather."

"Good heavens!" she exclaimed. "No way you're going to get out of cooking what you promised."

He relaxed a little bit, but eyed her now and then, from where he knelt by the fire stirring up the coals, and adding more wood before he put the meat on to cook. He looked at the two chairs she kept near the door for putting on the porch or at the table and finally said, "Brock told me that I was all kinds of a fool for letting you sca—uh—trick me that way."

Lorrie had to bite the inside of her upper lip to keep from laughing. She finally said, "Gray Cloud could hardly keep up with you." And she put her hand over her mouth to keep from laughing aloud.

The mountain man flushed, which made her realize that he was clean shaven. He hadn't regrown his beard out in the wild. "A storm caught us one day before I'd had time to throw together a shelter, but we found a deadfall to shelter in. I swear Gray Cloud looked at me and shook his head before burying his head under his tail."

"Why?"

"Because I was still running and not paying attention; we could have been warm inside a cabin instead. As I laid there, for the first time, I thought how cozy a cabin would be, but then I realized I wasn't missing a cabin. I was missing you." That took her aback, and she couldn't think of anything funny—or protective—to say.

He walked to the door and looked out. Gray Cloud watched him with interest, but didn't stir from the rug in front of the chair facing the fireplace. He turned back and faced her. "Another thing Brock told me when I stopped by his cabin earlier, was that he thought that one reason you chased me off was so I wouldn't bother you, when you took off on one of your trips, which you didn't mention to me."

"Why should I? A long time ago, a man told me that I needed a man to take care of me, and that made me angry, partly because I realized that

I'd been relying on my uncle to take care of me up to then. I've made sure since then, that no one would even think they had to take care of me, especially when I was so good at taking care of them. The thought of you telling me not to go—or that you'd go or someone else could go—made me angry all over again."

"I wouldn't," he said. He looked at the wolf, "If I ever do that, you bite me. You bite me good!"

"And I'll hit you with a frying pan," she promised. "Are you thinking of building a cabin here? Of home-steading?"

He frowned. "I hadn't thought that far," and he looked around her cabin thoughtfully. So, she thought, maybe he hadn't thought beyond her cabin—and her.

He flushed again when he caught her studying him. "I wasn't thinking of..." He stopped, confused. "What do you think?"

"I want to know what you think," she told him. "I'm not sure you've been thinking. You've just been feeling, which isn't a bad thing, if you know…" Now she was a little confused. She did know that this wasn't how a man courted a woman.

"I think I'm going to run up the mountain," he said. And he was out the cabin door and off the porch in one bound and before long he'd disappeared into the woods.

Lorrie looked at Gray Cloud. "You go with him. I don't want him thinking he has to come back for you." The wolf rose and trotted out the door. Last thing she saw of him, he was running into the woods.

Lorrie was relieved to be alone. Now she could think. Think about him. About how she felt about him. She'd never felt the wild passion that she read about in the novels she sometimes read during the winter nights. She'd felt contentment sitting beside him on the porch when he was getting his strength back. And the only man she had to compare him to, was Bolt. She liked Bolt, his quiet strength, the way he moved, the way he didn't feel the need to protect her from going into danger, but being there when she needed him, and his sense of humor. She wasn't sure Barrett had a sense of humor.

The air was changing from cool to cold, and she was about to give up and go back into the cabin and at least get a blanket when he and the wolf were beside her on the porch. "It wasn't that I didn't think about you before," he said; "I felt good just sitting next to you, and you only cared about me getting better and going back to the woods. I thought about touching you, but I knew I'd scare you, and that would be the end of the porch sitting, and I didn't want Brock to kill me."

Oh, maybe he did have a sense of humor after all. And he could cook. She might be one of the few women who'd take that into consideration. "Are you sure?" She didn't want a man who had to be dragged into marriage like a horse being dragged into the corral to be broken. "You don't want to take another year or two to make up your mind for certain?"

"No, I'm sure, and it suddenly dawned on me that while I'm being scared and stupid, another man could claim you and be the one to touch you. Now that truly scares me."

And what came out of her mouth next startled them both. "You can touch me," and she didn't say it hesitantly. It was an invitation. He picked her up and took her into the cabin and held her closely in the light of the fire. Hugging and kissing standing up led to hugging and kissing and more touching lying on the floor.

The dying fire was casting shadows and the occasional spark when he finally raised himself up and rested on his arms over her, studying her face. "Oh, good," she said. "Maybe I won't need the skillet after all."

He shook his head and laughed. "Nope. I'm due at the Summers' to spend the night there. And I wouldn't be surprised if Brock came to fetch me. But wait a minute, I'm trying to think of the words."

"Words?"

"Will you marry me?"

Was she sure? She needed to be sure. On the other hand, you can't leave a man dangling like this. "Yes," she breathed. What came next? "But there is no minister here yet."

"We're not going to wait for a minister to come here?!" The man was sounding more and more certain.

"No. Now that is for sure. We can go to Rocky Falls or farther up or down the trail, but my family, my friends are here. They can't just pack up and come. So, I'll go find one, and I'll take the small wagon for supplies at the same time. That'll be quicker, and I won't waste the trip."

Barrett was startled at that, but it was a hint of the woman that Brock had spoken to him so firmly about. "I don't know if she'll have you," he'd said, "but if she does, don't you ever try to hobble her."

Chapter Fourteen
~ Family Ties ~

Impatient as they both were—finally—Lorrie was glad for the time to talk to the women in her life. Her family. The trip was put off a little longer while they studied the clothes and materials available. "Back in the old times," Hannah said, "I was a seamstress. I haven't done much since but mending, but the lavender silk will make a lovely dress. I think a white silk sash and this white lace for a veil."

"I've got white gloves—long ones," Elizabeth Johnson put in.

"Don't we need something blue?" asked Carrol. She'd begun thinking of weddings more with Lorrie's coming up. "And we'll have garden flowers for the bouquet."

"Be sure to bring back some fancy food for the wedding," Elizabeth reminded her, when she finally set off with Dennis and Carrol. They'd said—she's our aunt; we have the right to go. The groom has to stay and build on the barn for more stock.

The trip to Rocky Falls was light-hearted, though all three stayed alert and kept their guns close by, while Jake trotted loosely alongside—sometimes.

They stayed at the Rocky Falls hotel as usual. Carrol and Dennis went to the general store, and Lorrie went straight to Territory Tales.

Ink was sitting on his desk with his feet on his chair this time, and shuffling sheets of paper—not newsprint—notes, she thought. "Busy as usual," she said.

He jumped off his desk to greet her, carefully avoiding brushing against her. His sleeves were ink-stained, as usual. "And full of news," he said. "I'm glad you're here because Nancy Chandler, you remember the reporter who was thinking of writing a book about you—and, of course, your settlement. Well, anyway, I got a letter from her a couple weeks ago that said she was coming out here in a few months, and it was on its way so long that she could be here anytime. And I was thinking I had to send out my reporters to look for you, so I'm glad you're in town. More supplies? Already?"

"No," she said, blushing a little. "I'm looking for a minster to come to Sugar Valley. Can you recommend one?"

"We have two, which is a good number for a town this size. I'd recommend Reverend Hendricks; he's more fit for the ride. Whose wedding? Yours?"

"Yes," she said and couldn't help smiling.

"Now there's a lucky man. And is it going to be big, fancy wedding?"

"If my friends have anything to say about it, I expect so."

"Oh, Lorrie, can I cover it? I could use a fancy wedding. I need more women readers; they'd love to read about something more exciting than their daily lives. Not that I blame them. I spend a lot of time looking for something exciting for the paper."

Lorrie shook her head. "I don't have a craving to be in your paper, Ink. I suppose some people may."

"You'd better believe it, but they don't have anything to contribute that readers would care about. And I want pictures."

Lorrie frowned. She didn't want pictures of her in the paper. In the future it might not be a good thing for anyone she met to recognize her. "I don't think so…"

"Lorrie, you want more settlers don't you? You've gone looking for them before, and your town doesn't even have a minister. Do you have a church?"

"Not yet," she admitted.

"This would bring some in. On your trips, you never even mention the name of your settlement. Heck, I only learned it from you not that long ago. I had picked up some word of Sugar Valley, but I couldn't be sure it was your town."

He switched subjects to give her time to think. "Who's the lucky man? Can I at least mention his name in the paper? I mean you have to tell the minister—and put an announcement in the newspaper after all."

"I never think of things like that out here," she confessed. "His name is Barrett Lee."

Ink made a mental note so he wouldn't spook her. He'd get the right spelling later. "And what does he do? Does he live in town?"

She flushed a little and could have kicked herself. "He's a mountain man. I have no idea where he's from."

"Papers usually want that information, but as you say, out here it doesn't matter so much." She smiled at him gratefully and flushed again.

"Wait a minute. Barett Lee. Why does that name sound familiar? But that Lee's not a mountain man. He's a scout. He's scouted for the fort and a few wagon trains. Did you ever ask him about his background? Where he's from?"

"No," she confessed. "I assumed…I couldn't ask him. I didn't even think of asking him!"

"Hmm. It seems to me, girl that you should find out about him. What's more, you should care about finding out more." He paused. "Sorry, it must be my newspaper training. I didn't mean to lecture you."

She shrugged. "Why not? Everyone else does. You must all think I'm ignorant."

"Nope. Just busy, though you haven't given me any news for a while. So, I'll bring Toby Kelly, the photographer, too. When is the wedding?"

"In the fall, after harvest. That way we can get everything finished and ready for winter."

"Ah, good plan. You don't have a date?" Ink was curious and already setting type in his mind.

"I thought it would depend on the minister. I wasn't sure how long it would take to track one down." Sometimes Lorrie couldn't wait, and sometimes she was just plain nervous. Hannah and Elizabeth Johnson took turns reassuring her—and gently explaining things she needed to know.

Before they left town, the three from Sugar Valley had filled the small wagon with a variety of supplies, and Lorrie promised Ink that she'd send word about the date when it was decided upon. It was Reverend Hendricks who coaxed her into committing to a date. It couldn't be too late, he pointed out, because of the possibility of an early snow. Mid October. October 14, he convinced her, would be a good date, and she should send him word if she changed her mind. He decided that the prospective groom wasn't too involved in the decision.

After returning home, Lorrie became so busy with wedding plans and preparations that the time flew. It reminded her of the first year they had prepared for winter. So much to do, including fittings for her wedding dress and a trousseau. Elizabeth set her husband to work to prepare the groom. "Just don't frighten him. We don't want him to get away now that Lorrie has finally decided to try domesticity."

"Is she going to cook?" he said, grinning.

Elizabeth laughed. "I'm going to be careful not to frighten her, either," she said firmly.

The minister arrived on October 12, and stayed at the Carruthers' hotel, along with Ink and his photographer, Kelly. They shared a wagon with the photo equipment and some packages. The wedding would be held at the hotel; the addition gave them room for dancing, which would be an important part of the festivities, and more guests would be arriving because Lorrie and Elizabeth had decided that this would an opportunity to introduce visitors to Sugar Valley and their eligible boys and girls.

October 14 dawned clear and cool, and gifts soon filled the hotel lobby. Lorrie was amazed and tried to check out the array of big and small packages, but Lizzie shooed her away. "Not until after the wedding," she said. "No one‘s going to relax until you‘re hitched. Then we all have fun, and you two will have to wait to have your fun later." Lorrie blushed, and Lizzie took hold of both her hands. "There's nothing to be afraid of. Keep your skillet by the bed, if you think you'll need it."

The wedding was scheduled for ten o'clock in the morning so everyone would have the rest of the day to meet and mingle. The dancing would start in the evening. The ceremony took place in the lobby; the town's womenfolk had draped it with lace and banners, and filled it with fall flowers and foliage. Lorrie thought she'd never seen anything more beautiful, and her friends standing in the lobby surrounding her made her feel even more safe and loved. Barrett was standing at the table in front of the hotel desk. He looked sleek and handsome and ready to be married, which was more important.

She shivered a little, but didn't hesitate. It was not necessary for Samuel Johnson to hold her arm tightly in case she tried to get away, but she was glad that she'd had so much experience in charging ahead and not running for cover. Barrett held out his hand, and now she pulled away to take it. She heard the minister's words, but remembered them more clearly afterwards. “I now pronounce you husband and wife,” did stand out though, as did Barrett’s careful, gentle embrace and kiss. He was surprised that it was he who was more worried about the wedding taking place than she. He guessed that meant that he was ready.

Afterwards there were drinks, meats, bread, and cake to follow. With stomachs filled, attention turned towards the gifts. The Johnsons gave them sheets; Hannah a newly-made quilt. “I know you have plenty of covers, but this is for you both to start out with.” There was food for the pantry; moccasins from Many Stars; a buckskin jacket from Brock; and a bed stuffed with rags for Gray Cloud that had been made by the Johnson children. When Rollie proudly pointed out the neat stitches he’d sewn for Gray Cloud (Sallie Sue wasn’t much of a seamstress), the wolf’s head popped out of the wrappings beside the table.

Lorrie was overwhelmed by the cornucopia of gifts surrounding her. She stood up at last and thanked them. “This, the happiest day of my life, has been enriched by your presence and your love.” She laughed and spelled the word so they wouldn‘t misunderstand it. Then came the dancing, and it kept on until the lanterns burned down and the fiddle players drooped. Families and couples strolled home, and as Lorrie and Barrett headed for the door, she saw that the gifts, the wrappings, and the food had disappeared. “Dennis took everything up in the wagon earlier,” Elizabeth told her, smothering a yawn, “so you didn’t have to think about it. Good-night you two; I hope to see you sometime during the next few days.”

Lorrie didn’t catch what she meant until they were riding up the trail, and she blushed, glad that her husband couldn’t see it. Thank heavens she was too tired to be nervous about what happened in their cabin. Their cabin. She mouthed the words. Not mine anymore. Was she sorry about that? It was all her hard work. Well, she’d had help. She was grateful for the long ride to sort out her feelings.

“Go on in,” he told her when they got home. Home. “I’ll take care of the horses.” Jake followed them to the barn in hopes of getting some oats, and Gray Cloud trailed behind. She had the cabin to herself. She felt her way to the lantern and lit it. The gifts were piled on the bed so she started putting them away. Everything going to the loft went by the ladder. He could carry them up. Ah, sharing chores was nice, she thought. She made the bed with the new sheets and put the old bed covers aside so that the new quilt went on top of the sheets.

She was stowing the food in the pantry, but she stopped when he came in and put the leftover wedding cake on the table. "I thought—since it's almost dawn—we could have cake for breakfast." He nodded and went to the well for cold water to wash it down with. Gray Cloud nosed his bed, but decided it was too warm in the cabin and went to the door. "I'll put his bed on the porch so if he gets cold he can use it," she told Barrett when he returned with a bucket of water. She cast about in her mind for more conversation.

"I'm tuckered out," he told her, so she wouldn't worry. She looked like a scared fawn that'd lost its mother. He took his boots off, and then his shirt, and then his pants. "I know you don't want the sheets to get dirty. You can come to bed when you're ready."

Lorrie was torn between relief and puzzlement. Was this how it was supposed to be? Then she remembered Hannah's reassuring words, "I think he's worried about you, so I don't think you need worry about him being rough. You may even need to encourage him."

So she'd do that, but not tonight; she was too tired to worry any more, and she changed into her nightie in a dark corner before joining him in bed. "Are you warm enough?" he said sleepily, making sure she was covered with the bedclothes. Lorrie fell asleep feeling coddled.

The room was bright in the morning with the door wide open and Gray Cloud curled up on the door sill. Bacon was frying, and there was a clatter of dishes on the table. She turned over and saw him pouring water in the wooden cups on the table and adding potatoes to the skillet. Oh, this was nice, and she smiled happily at him. He smiled back, put the pan to the side of the fire and joined her in bed.

He wrapped her in the sheet and held her while he nuzzled her neck and kissed her face and neck, and then he unwrapped her completely, and she was lost in a haze of feelings and touchings and respondings and fulfillment. She was glad they hadn't waited any longer. 'Course they both had been unready, but that time was gone.

When they ran out of food in the cabin, she rode Jake with his pack saddle to the valley, and Barrett went hunting with Cloud. Lizzie didn't seem surprised that she'd only come to the general store now. Usually Lorrie went down every other day for a meal. "How did you like the sheets?"

Lorrie looked her in the eye and said, "Those are the best sheets I ever slept with—uh, I mean in." But she didn't blush.

"You're happy then, girl?"

"Of course, and he makes me breakfast and lunch and supper." Lorrie knew that was a lot to grateful for.

"He is a paragon then! But you've got to carry your share of the load," she reminded her.

"I will. I'm going to make bread while he's out hunting, and I am milking the cows and taking care of my chores."

"And sometimes you'll do his." Elizabeth wasn't about to stop teaching the girl who was used to having her own way, that things were different now.

Chapter Fifteen
~ Starting a Family ~

Lorrie was well aware that things were different, which is why she sat thoughtfully on the porch in the afternoon sun one day and decided not to tell her husband that she might be pregnant. Even her paragon might become possessive of his family, and she had been planning the trip to Fort Laramie for two months. She wanted to take Dennis, Carrol, and Star to meet people of the opposite sex whom they didn't know.

Cloud hadn't bothered to follow his companion to the smokehouse after their hunting trip, but now he sat up and stared intently up the mountain trail so Lorrie wasn't surprised to see two strangers emerge from the woods. A man and a little boy, obviously not a threat, especially since Jake was trailing them. Cloud jumped off the porch and headed for the smokehouse since Jake was there on guard.

Barrett came running up the path, but stopped when he saw the visitors. The two men greeted each other quietly. The boy stood silent and still and distant. The two men looked at him, then they walked around him and came to where she sat on the porch. "Lorrie, this is my friend, Manfred Dennison. "Manny, this is my wife, Lorrie Lee. Lorrie, Manny has come down from the mountains to ask for my help. For our help. You tell her, Manny."

"Mrs. Lee, my son, Davy, has lost his mother." He paused, but Lorrie didn't think it was to give her a chance to express effusive condolences.

She said only, "I'm so sorry to hear it, Mr. Dennison," and waited for him to continue. However, he stood mute for several minutes staring at the ground. Lorrie glanced at Barrett for direction, but he shook his head, so they both waited.

"My wife, Blue Sky, was murdered. They hurt her bad. The boy was with me so he didn't see it. They might have killed him too, if he'd been there, so I was glad for that. Now I've got to track them down and kill them; taking him would slow me down, and I wouldn't want him to see me do it because it's not going to be a clean kill, and I want him taken care of and safe if things go badly for me."

"Barr, I see you and your wife don't like the idea, but think about what you'd do if someone ripped up your woman."

"Thinking about that, Manny, tempts me to join you except for the need to stay and care for them. And I see the need to be more careful of what I have to lose."

Manfred turned to Lorrie, "You don't mind Mrs. Lee, taking care of a half-breed?" And he watched her closely for signs of unease.

"Mr. Dennison, one of my best friends, Starlight, is a half-breed, though I never use that word myself." He heard the distaste in her tone and was reassured.

He turned to the boy, who stood apart and watchful. "Hey, Davy, come over here and meet my friends."

Lorrie asked softly, "Does he know about his mother?"

"He knows she was murdered, but no details. When I saw her lying there in the cabin," and he swallowed and choked, but continued quickly, "I told him to take care of the horses and furs. And I wrapped her up and buried her like that so he was there to see her laid to rest, but would remember her as he'd last seen her."

Lorrie nodded in agreement and then sat down on the porch steps as the boy approached, his hair black and long and uncombed and his body and clothes dirty from the trail. "Would you like to stay with us while your father goes back on the trail?" Well, that was dumb, she thought. Why would he? So she sat quietly and left it to the men.

Manny glanced at her before he knelt beside his son. "She wants you to feel welcomed," he told him, "but you know that you have to stay with my friends 'til I come back for you. I can't promise you when I'll be back; I can't even promise you that I'll come back, because you know how things can chance on the trail, and I never promised you anything I couldn't keep. It's about a man keeping his word. I always taught you that."

The boy looked up at his father, and Lorrie saw the trust in his eyes. "I'll always keep my word too, father," he promised.

Manny smiled, happy for a moment in his son, and then he said slowly, "That's why I want you to promise me that you'll stay here. It may not always be easy, but you know that you have to take the rough with the smooth."

"Of course, you and mother taught me that, too." His mouth quivered for a moment, and his father reached out and hugged him, rocking back and forth until at last, he rose, and said, "I have to go now before the trail gets cold."

"Supper?" But he shook his head at her and turned away, heading for the woods. Barrett caught up with him before he reached the shade of the trees and handed him a sack.

"I gave him bread and meat so he wouldn't go hungry on the trail," he told Davy and Lorrie. She nodded. Her husband was a thoughtful and careful man, and he was now a lot less likely to let her go off on her own.

The first thing Lorrie did was to introduce Davy to Jake and Gray Cloud, and while he was engrossed in talking to them and hugging them, possibly more so than he might have done if he hadn't just lost his mother, she drew Barrett aside. "He can sleep in the loft, of course, my old mattress is up there, and he'll need a chest. You can take the little one up later."

"Why?"

"Because he's going to need clothes, and you'll have to cut his hair too."

Her husband eyed her. "Is he too wild-looking?" He was disappointed in her, and she was impatient with him.

"He's going to live here," she pointed out. 'Do you plan to keep him away from everyone? And what about us?"

"Us?" She didn't stamp her foot, but he saw that she was tempted and put his mind to work. "Ah, I see." He went and stood in the cabin door, and she knew he was looking at their big bed in the back corner of the one room cabin.

"We haven't been married for all that long," she said, as if he might not have remembered, "and I still look forward to going to bed—early."

He smiled and touched her cheek. "Early or late or mid-morning, as I recall."

"Well, it was just a matter of time, after all," she said, suddenly cheerful.

"Oh?" he said, cautiously.

"It's time to add on to the cabin. Two more rooms, I think."

"Two?"

"We need room for the furniture—some of the things I still have stored at the Johnsons, though now everything's in their new barn—up in the loft."

"What? Why?" She'd confused him so she'd give him a hint.

"We'll need a bigger table, more chairs, and beds, and chests." She didn't mention the cradle.

Except for Davy, they didn't go to bed early that night. Chores in the barn kept them busy after Barrett had checked to see the boy was asleep. "He's completely tuckered out," her husband reported. "He and I will wash up in the morning, and then I'll cut his hair."

She nodded. "And then I'll take him to town to get clothes and introduce him. I'll stop to see Hannah, Evan, Carrol, and Michael on the way back. We'll probably eat a little here and there so he feels welcome every place."

"Any chance he won't feel welcome?" he wondered uneasily.

"Oh, no," she told him, and he felt more confident then too. Lorrie gradually learned that Davy was almost eight years old and his father had taught him to read and write—a little. The boy stayed to himself the first couple days, feeling most comfortable with the mule and the wolf, but when he began to trust them, she took him to visit what she considered her extended family.

Lorrie spent the next week making the rounds of the valley with Davy and altering her plans. The kids would have to find their own friends. She couldn't do everything, but as the day came for which she was still planning, Ink arrived with the reporter from the big city.

She couldn't help smiling when she saw him and the young woman. They rode up to the cabin, and he swung down and gave his companion a hand. "Lorrie," he said brightly, "This is Nancy Chandler. Miss Chandler, this is Lorena Lee." Nancy Chandler was beside herself with delight, and Lorrie wondered at her enthusiasm.

"Mrs. Lee, I appreciate your taking the time to talk to me. And I hope you'll let me take some photos of you. And Gray Cloud and Jake and your husband, your cabin, the valley."

"I'll have to see if they're all agreeable," she said. "Uh, where is your camera?"

The reporter grew serious. "I was not planning to take you unawares," she assured her. I left the cameras, the photographer and even my notebooks back at the hotel. We came by wagon to carry everything. You don't mind about us taking the photos?"

"No," Lorrie told her. "I've been thinking that I'd like to have copies of all those photos myself. You can bring the photographer up tomorrow to give me time to round everyone up."

"Where are they?" the reporter wondered.

Lorrie looked behind her to where Jake and Davy were standing and watching. "I suspect Jake followed you in."

"Nancy Chandler turned around to see what Lorrie was looking at and smiled to see the big mule so close. Then she looked at Davy. "Uh, is this one of yours?" She glanced at Ink, who shrugged and looked ignorant.

"Yes, he's a member of the family now. He lost his mother, and his father is elsewhere. I'll want a picture of him too, of course."

Nancy brought the photographer the next day, and Lorrie persuaded her husband to have his picture taken with Gray Cloud, then her, then the four of them, then the five of them, and also Sunny and Shadow, the cabin, the barn.... Eventually, Nancy and the photographer escaped, and the reporter spent the next week talking to everyone in the valley and on the hillside. She returned periodically to ask Lorrie to confirm facts and anecdotes in her notebooks.

"So, you brought the Carruthers here, and the blacksmith, after the first group settled here? You led them here?"

"No," Lorrie hastened to correct her. "We all made the decision, and Mr. Brown was the wagon master of our little train, and Mr. Summers was our guide, and Mrs. Johnson and baby Sarah were mostly responsible for the decision to stop here. Please do not say that I was responsible or in charge."

Nancy made another note. "I promise," she told her. "What about the others who are here now?"

"I found the mason at Fort Laramie. Others heard about us from the fort and nearby towns and Mr. Matthews and his stories in his paper, I think. And some people apparently just wandered in from passing wagon trains. Some settlers wrote to family and friends, and I never expected to grow so quickly 'cause we started slow. The general store helped, of course. People started coming here for supplies, and I, that is, we, had to keep it stocked."

Nancy nodded and turned the page to make more notes. Lorrie thought she was on her fourth notebook. Lorrie had begun to expect to see Nancy every day, and Barr and Davy took to vanishing every time Jake stared down the trail. Finally, one day, Nancy rode up and didn't take out her notebook or settle on the porch to talk. She walked around the cabin, patted Shadow, who was taking her turn in the corral, and hugged Jake.

Lorrie waited on the porch, allowing her to make her rounds alone, and she wasn't surprised when Nancy came to her, and said, "I've stayed as long as I can. The photographer is itching to go home and develop the plates, and I have to get to work on my book. I hope I haven't been too much of a nuisance."

Lorrie shook her head decisively. "No, as a matter of fact, I'm going to miss you. Maybe you'll come back when your book is done so I can see it."

"Of course. I'll send you copies of the book and the photos, if I can't come myself then. There may be book tours then," she added.

Lorrie nodded. Book tours, huh. She merely hoped the book didn't stray too far from truth. Nancy turned and hugged her tightly before she mounted her horse, and Lorrie hugged her back. Nancy turned her horse in a circle, and came back. "I won't disappoint you," she said.

She meant it, Lorrie saw and was relieved. Now she probably wouldn't have to track all those book copies down and burn them. After that, she turned her attention to her husband. "Well, I don't think it's too early," she said firmly, "but if they don't have hay, get oats or something. I want to be sure they don't sell it all to the fort. Dennis will drive the big wagon with Abe and Sarah." Before they left, she said to Dennis, "Don't hurry back if you want to spend some time with one of the Hanson girls."

"You and Carrol," he said, "always trying to match me up with some girl," but he appeared to be looking forward to the trip. After they were gone, she packed Davy's clothes in a satchel and took him to Hannah's cabin.

Hannah was shelling beans on her front porch. "Okay, Davy, you're going to stay with Aunt Hannah while I'm gone. I told him to help you and Evan with chores," she told her. "If he has time, because he's got to take care of our place too. Do you think you can do that, Davy?" she asked him.

"Of course I can," he affirmed. He'd been pleased to learn he was in charge of his home, but relieved that he wouldn't be staying there alone at night. Lorrie bent over and hugged him, and he held her tightly for a moment before stepping back. He looked a little lonely when she looked searchingly at him, but then he straightened up and tilted his chin. "Show me where I should put my stuff," he said to Hannah. Both Hannah and Lorrie looked at him sharply. "Please, ma'am," he added quickly. "Please."

Lorrie turned away and went swiftly back to her cabin. If there'd been time, she'd have hugged him again. Star should be joining her there soon, though. She'd persuaded her father to convince her mother that it was time she went back into the world again. "You know I have to go out there, and besides, Lorrie needs me."

"I'm surprised that Barrett is letting her go off on her own," was all he said when she took her clothes, gun, and knife and left. If he thought different, he didn't let on.

Lorrie and Star rode down to the general store and sent Jake after Sunny; then they hitched Sunny and Shadow to the small wagon with Jake and Swift trailing behind. With Jake at hand, Star didn't see the need to put her horse on a long line.

With Barr heading west, Lorrie headed east. She'd decided to go through Lotawater and stop at Wayside to see what the town had and to visit old friends. They stopped at Lotawater to eat and rest the horses, and see what changes there might be there. Even Jake didn't see the man who started when he saw Lorrie and slunk around a corner, holding his maimed hand, a habit he'd mostly gotten rid of.

They were over halfway to Wayside, walking the team slowly down a steep grade when a man rode out from behind the rocks; he was holding a rifle and had a tight bead on the two women. Lorrie pulled the team up, looked back into the wagon and yelled, "Get 'em, Jake!"

As Colly spurred his horse forward to get a clear shot at the wagon, Jake blindsided him, knocking him off his horse on the road. Jake wheeled and was coming back when Colly fired, nicking Sunny. The mare screamed, and the team leaped forward as one, running over the man lying in front of them.

It took Lorrie and Star several minutes hauling on the reins before they were able to stop the horses. "Check out Sunny, Star. I'm going back for Jake," and she unhitched Shadow and mounted her bareback, not wanting to waste time. Sunny'd be less likely to run again by herself, which should make it easier for Star.

She was back on the scene shortly, having kept Shadow at a run, but Jake was just keeping an eye on the man. She couldn't tell if he had stomped him or not. He might have. Too hard to tell, she hoped. No way of telling what story someone will make out of this, she mused, as she headed back.

"How's Sunny?" Lorrie asked, swinging down from Swift's back. Star had unhitched her, too, and was applying salve to a bloody gash on her flank.

"Not too bad, but I don't think she should pull. Let's try Swift with Shadow. She's not trained to pull a wagon, but I think I can settle her down, if I need to. I prefer having Jake loose."

"Oh, yes. We'll see how she does on a long line. We're going straight to the marshal's office," Lorrie said decisively.

Lorrie wasn't sure Bolt would be in his office, but she certainly hadn't expected to see him changing a baby's diaper on his desk. "I have to report a dead man back on the trail," she told him.

"You do it?"

"Nope. Well, not exactly. It was Colly, and he tried to hold us up on the trail. He shot at us and hit one of my horses, and the team spooked and ran him over. I don't know how he knew we'd be along." That puzzled her.

Bolt finished with the baby and placed him gently in a deep desk drawer. "I ran him out of town again, and last I heard he was in Lotawater. You passed through there, I 'spect."

Lorrie nodded. "And stopped for a while. I'm glad it's you. Might be hard to explain to a stranger."

"I'll send a deputy to bring the body in. Thanks for reporting it, by the way. Saves me time and trouble." He went to the door and whistled. "Stay for a minute and tell the deputy," he said, smiling. A tall, young man raced in the door.

"What is it, Bolt?!"

"Look who's here, Jason," and he laughed when he saw the surprise on Lorrie's face.

"Jason," she said. "You've grown!"

"In body and mind and skill," Bolt said, suddenly serious. "You left me the best pair any marshal could have asked for. Tim's out of town, or I'd call him in, too. Okay, Jason, she's done it again. There's a body back along the trail. And guess who. Colly."

"You shoot him again?"

She shook her head. "Too slow. I didn't have my gun in my hand, and he had the drop on me, so I had to use horses." They all laughed. There aren't many, Lorrie thought, that I could joke with about this.

With Jason on his way, Lorrie looked at the baby in the drawer. "Yours?"

"Yep." Bolt sat down on the floor to admire the baby. "His mother's substitute teaching this week because the current teacher is about to have a baby. We're all waiting for the next one to arrive on the stage. How about you? Married?"

Lorrie blushed and nodded. "And," she said, "I have a boy who's older than yours."

He looked up at her and laughed. "Only you."

Lorrie grinned, then bent over the baby, who was slowly falling asleep, stirring now and then to wave his hands about. "What's his name?" she asked softly.

"Marcus. He's named after Victoria's grandfather. Marcus Andrew Saunders."

Lorrie stood up and moved away so she wouldn't keep little Marcus awake with talking. "After his grandfather. I haven't even thought about names yet. That's a good idea. I have to find out, uh, names." She remembered what Brock had said about finding out more about Barrett. She'd do that when she went back. She sighed.

Marshal Saunders looked at her, and she remembered having heard the name in town, but she would always think of him as Bolt. Now Bolt waited to hear what she was thinking. She looked at him. "I would like to meet Victoria," she told him.

He was curious, but only said, "We can ride out to the school soon. Marcus and I'll be picking her up in the buggy. He's only here 'cause Mrs. Granger dropped him off on her way to deliver a baby. Wayside is growing fast, and the town council plans to rename it as soon as they can agree on a name!"

Lorrie laughed and nodded and went on to explain, in case he was wondering what she wanted. “I’ve talked to women back home about, well, birthing babies, but it’s fresh in her mind, and she could maybe give me some hints. As a matter of fact, I’m in town to buy a cradle; I left Star with the wagon at the general store to look around after we took Sunny to the livery stable to have her wound taken care of.”

Bolt nodded. “Why don’t you go there, and I’ll pick you up in an hour or so.” Lorrie agreed and looked around as she made her way up the street. New boardwalks. Sugar Valley needed those now. More horses at the hitching racks and more buggies stirring up dust. Sugar Valley had a ways to go to reach this point, and she was glad.

The store was dark after the bright sunlight outside, and Lorrie paused to let her eyes adjust before she looked for Star. In a minute she saw her. Backed up against the store counter; she looked beleaguered, and Lorrie circled so as to come up behind the women facing her.

“Whad’cha let a half-breed in your store for, Josh?” The old woman—no, maybe not so old, had apparently stopped to take a breath and was renewing her attack, it looked like.

The man behind the counter was looking a bit beleaguered, too. “Her money’s good,” he said feebly, looking around hopelessly. The woman, gray hair straggling out from under a faded bonnet, looked around, grabbed a long package from on the counter and hefted it as if about to strike.

Lorrie was sorry it wasn’t a man she had to deal with, but that didn’t stop her from moving silently forward, wresting the package from the woman’s hand, tossing it to the far end of the counter, and placing herself in front of Star. “Why for you attacking my sister, granny?” she demanded and moved forward to stop only a couple inches from her foe.

“Sister?!” the woman screeched, spittle sprinkling Lorrie’s face. She managed not to flinch or wipe her face. She’d wash up later. “You one of them Injun lovers?!”

Lorrie found herself getting impatient. She hadn’t felt the urge to attack since…well, actually it was this morning, but this couldn’t be allowed to end the same way. She shook her head and braced herself to move forward a little more.

“Ladies, ladies!” The man behind the counter was sweating. He looked at one of the women standing silently in the frozen tableau. “Cassie, take your mother home, please.” Then he turned to Lorrie, “She lost her husband and two children in an Indian attack down south last year. You can't blame her for being, uh, excitable."

Lorrie relaxed and felt a stirring of sympathy. "I am sorry, ma'am. I understand now. I had to take some arrows out of my man not so long ago. I almost lost him." She skipped unabashedly over the exact facts. "'Course the only men who ever attacked me were white men..." She trailed off because she couldn't decide where to go with that thought. "Howsomever, that don't give you the right to attack my sister, when we only was in town to get a cradle for my baby." And she patted her stomach. She'd felt sympathy herself when learning the facts. Maybe that would work on the old woman. It didn't.

While she sputtered and snarled, and Cassie had begun tugging, fruitlessly, on her arm, one of the other women spoke out with unabashed curiosity. "How is she your sister?"

Lorrie turned to her with relief. "I have a very large and curious family. We've taken each other in and helped when needed, especially the womenfolk, because...I guess because that's what women do." She did not add—and we bash folks who need bashing. She turned to Star, putting her back to the other woman and hoping those surrounding her would help as needed. "Did you find a cradle, Star?"

Star gave a tentative nod, but didn't stir, and the man came from around the counter, evidently not feeling the need of its protection as much now. "Yes, she did. I have three to choose from, if you'll come this way," and he backed away from the old woman, not as trusting as Lorrie. The other women, four, Lorrie noticed, as one emerged from the shadows where she'd taken shelter, surrounded the widow and herded her out. Lorrie heard her weeping on her way to the door.

Josh wiped his brow with a sodden handkerchief and apologized. "You understand, I'm sure, but I'm sorry for your trouble." He sighed. "Her husband was my brother," he added, "and I think she's sorry that it wasn't me, instead of him they killed. But I was in town in the store, and he was bringing back a load of supplies."

"I see," Lorrie said. "We haven't had much Indian trouble—not lately. They're mostly south and west, I understand."

"You can never tell where they'll turn up," he said vaguely, looking away from Star. "But let's look at those cradles now." He led them to a side room, full mostly of furniture and shelves of clothes. Lorrie was distracted by a shelf of baby clothes, and after deciding on two cradles because they didn't have any back home, went back to looking through the clothes. She was sitting on the floor holding two little dresses when Bolt arrived.

"Most women make their own, you know, but we found these back in Independence and took a chance. I'm glad you like them." Lorrie wondered if the we referred to him and his brother but didn't ask. The storekeeper looked up. "Hi, Marshal. Need something?"

"Nope, but thank you, Mr. Wendell. I'm just here to pick up my friends." The storekeeper blinked, and Lorrie saw him absorbing the information. Shouldn't hurt to be the marshal's friend, she thought, to say nothing of the deputies'.

Bolt drove his buggy to the school while Lorrie carefully and tightly held little Marcus; she handed him down to Bolt after he jumped down, and they waited outside until the school began emptying. Bolt led the way inside, where a lone boy was industriously scrubbing the big blackboard, while a small blonde woman sat at the big desk near the wood stove, scribbling on papers. She looked up when they came in and her face lit up. "I'm almost done," she told Bolt before turning to the boy. "That's enough for now, Mike. Now, next time, be careful with the inkwells. They're not to be juggled. You'd be here all night scrubbing the floor if you'd dropped it," she said firmly.

"But I never do." She looked up at the ceiling and held back a smile.

The boy looked curiously at the visitors and dawdled on his way to the door. "Off with you now, Mikey."

He looked back at her in sudden chagrin. "I'm not Mikey. I'm Mike—or Michael!"

"Maybe," she said and paused, "when you stop juggling inkwells." He snorted and left.

She waited till the door closed behind him to laugh.

Lorrie saw Bolt smiling in appreciation. Then he moved forward to the desk, but stood on the other side, probably because of them, Lorrie thought. "Vicky, here is Lorrie Emerson, who wants to meet you, and her friend Star."

"I'm Lorrie Lee now," she said, "and I was admiring little Marcus earlier, and I thought I'd like to talk to you while I'm in town. I don't get here often." She turned to the other two. "Maybe you can show Star around outside. We're still working on our school. Maybe you can get some ideas for Sugar Valley, Star." Bolt handed the baby over to his mother. "I changed him again, before I left," he told her and escorted

Star outside.

Victoria studied Lorrie. “I’ve heard about you—a lot from Tim and Jason—until Bolt shushes them. You’re married now?”

“Yes, and pregnant. Mostly I’m too busy to think about it, and I’ve talked with mothers back home, but when I saw your baby, I suddenly felt I could learn a little more here, and Bolt let me hold him in the buggy, ’cause he was driving,” she hastened to add.

Vicky nodded, “Of course. You know he was scared to hold him at first, but now not so much. He’s always watchful, though.”

“Always,” Lorrie said, remembering.

“You knew him before I did. I confess I was a little jealous of you. You sounded so strong. You didn’t need him to protect you?”

“Of course I did. That’s how we met—and Timmy and Jason.”

“Tell me, please. I’ve always wanted to know, but he just smiles at me when I ask, and I forget.” She blushed.

“I needed his help,” she said, starting at the beginning. When she finished….

“Oh, I never would have done that. You didn’t even know him?!”

Lorrie shrugged. “Timmy and Jason recommended him. ’Course they knew he was the marshal, but I didn’t. But I liked him.” And she smiled, thinking back a little longer.

Vicky wondered what she remembered exactly, but she felt reassured anyway. “Tell me about your husband. Is he like Bolt?”

Lorrie considered. “Bolt is strong and good and ready to step in. And he’d tear apart any man who tried to hurt you.”

“Yes,” Vicky agreed. “Tell me about your husband. What’s his name? And is he very like Bolt?”

“His name is Barrett Lee, and I only recently found out that his nickname is Barr. He’s strong and good, and I suppose he’d kill anyone who tried to hurt me, but there never was the need. I’ve been careful about that. I even sent him away when I came here, and he doesn’t know I’m pregnant. I didn’t tell anyone, which I guess is one reason I wanted to talk to you. I wanted to tell someone. Back home they might have tried to persuade me not to go.”

“They wouldn’t stop you?”

Lorrie looked at her in surprise. “Never. And I didn’t want him to even think about it.”

Vicky thought about that. “I see. You don’t want him to take care of you?"

"Well, he does chores and cooks, and I told him we needed to add on to the cabin, but didn't say why. He finally guessed, I think."

"So they're sort of alike. Good men. Good husbands."

Lorrie had to laugh. "Actually Barr wasn't too keen on the idea at first. Fortunately for us both, neither was I."

Vicky looked at her in amazement and realization. "Bolt likes taking care of me, though I don't think he'd cook," she admitted. "You didn't want to be taken care of. At least you weren't ready."

Lorrie looked at Vicky. "I see." She didn't admit that she'd had family and a mule instead. "Are you out here by yourself? From back east? No family here?"

"No, they're all back east. Mother's afraid to come, and she won't let my sisters or brothers come."

"How'd you escape?"

"Mother was afraid, and I didn't want to be. And she'd picked out a man for me. He scared me to death! So I ran away. And I found Bolt, and I have Marcus. I think back to my home, and I shudder. Do you have family here?"

"Yes, but we joined together and became a family. Like you, I think back to my family back east and shudder. I also ran away, but with an uncle. He took care of me on the wagon train until he was killed. I wasn't like you. Not as brave as you."

Vicky sat back in her chair. "You think I'm brave?! I've been feeling so inadequate next to you."

Lorrie grinned. "You think Bolt would pick a person like that!" She laughed out loud. "I know he wouldn't."

Vicky sat up straight in her chair. "I'm so glad you came. I worry about Tim and Jason sometimes, wondering if they compare me to you."

"Hah! Don't. Always remember that they took care of me. I couldn't have done anything without their help along the way. Tell them that sometime—How I told you how I relied on them. And how you rely on all of them—to take care of each other. You don't have to think about them taking care of you. And you have a baby to take care of. Could they do that? Not likely. That would probably scare them silly."

"I miss my sisters sometimes. I hope you'll come back again." Lorrie thought of her sisters and family and her new son—all adopted. She hadn't thought of Davy as a son before—just someone to take care of. She didn't stop often enough to be grateful, she realized. For her family and for her husband. She wondered if she would have done as well as Vicky. Oh, probably.

"Of course, and our children can be cousins. I like that, Vicky. I hope you do. Interesting. I never wondered if Bolt had family—or Barr. Do you know?"

"He never talks about anyone," she said doubtfully. "He changes the subject when I ask."

"At least you ask. I have to be prodded by a friend to think of other people. I do care," she added, "I just don't think about it."

Star knocked on the door and stuck her head in. Bolt wants to know if you two plan to spend the night here. He's wondering what you're talking about, I think."

"And well he should," Lorrie said, giggling. Odd, she never giggled. Talking to Vicky was relaxing, she realized. At home, she had to be alert. But not here. Here, with the couple, that she now considered part of her family—plus little Marcus—she wasn't worrying about something or making plans.

Naturally, since it was getting late, Vicky invited them for supper, and Lorrie observed while Vicky put Marcus to bed. Supper was good; Vicky did all the cooking and served up steak, potatoes, baked beans, and bread, followed by blueberry pie for dessert. It was an enjoyable time for everyone, and Lorrie got a taste of home life as others lived it.

After spending the night at the hotel, Tim fetched her the next day to identify the body he'd brought back the day before. "That's him," she said, before turning quickly away, suddenly feeling nauseous.

She was waiting on the porch when Bolt joined her. "You all right?"

She looked at him, feeling a trifle embarrassed. "I think it's the baby."

"Oh," he said sympathetically. "I remember Vicky before the baby came. Be sure to pick out everything you can think of, at the general store. Vicky craved pickles sometimes, and then it was cheese, and once ice cream. We didn't even have a freezer then. I'll never be without one again!"

"I'd heard something about that," she remembered. "Thanks. I will buy more supplies before we leave, which will be soon. I'll stop by your house to say good-bye to Vicky and the baby. And please tell Jason that I'm sorry I missed him."

She and Vicky hugged, and Vicky had Lorrie hold Marcus for the practice. Lorrie was relieved to return him to his mother's arms. The two women hugged again while Star waited with the team and wagon out front. Vicky was reluctant to let Lorrie go. Lorrie realized that it probably wasn't just the fact that she had no family, but being the marshal's wife probably wasn't easy either.

Back on the road, she found herself looking forward to being in her own home. "I hope the trip wasn't too hard on you, Star, waiting while I visited."

Star shrugged and smiled. "I'm glad you got to see your friends, and it just makes me grateful that I have my own. I'm not going to tell Mother about the incident in the store. Please don't mention it to her."

"Of course not. She doesn't need to know. I'm sorry I couldn't do more there, but it wasn't a case of shooting someone who attacked you. That'd have been easier."

"And it was a good thing it didn't happen in the street, with me on the wagon holding the reins." Star smiled, albeit a little lopsided.

"Home is indeed looking good," Lorrie said.

Chapter Sixteen
~ Seasons Change ~

They drove the wagon up to Lorrie's cabin, where Davy ran to meet them. The sound of hammering brought them around behind the cabin, where men were working on a cabin addition. There were boards—real boards—piled to one side. Evan came out of the back door to greet them. "This is Mrs. Lee, men. Lorrie, here's Will Considine and his brother, Jimbo. Barr sent for them and they came up with the wood a few days ago."

Lorrie was stunned. The work begun so soon. Well, it was a good thing she was back to watch over the project. "I'll be right back," she told them and went back to the wagon where Star was unloading what she'd bought and packing it on Swift.

"I put Sunny in the corral and looked at the wound before I turned her loose; it's healing nicely. I think you can put her in the valley pasture soon. I left Shadow tied to the wagon tongue. Now I'm off, but I'll be back to look at the cabin as soon as I know Mother doesn't need me," she promised.

"Take your time, Star. I think she'll want you close to see that you're safe and sound; and I'll bring up anything of yours if I find it." Star nodded and gave a final tug on the pack saddles to see they were tight before swinging one leg carefully over the pack.

Lorrie watched her go and turned around to see Davy waiting by the wagon. "Are Dennis and Barr back yet?" she asked. She didn't see Jake. He was probably keeping an eye on the workmen.

"No, not yet. Can I get my stuff from the Browns' now?"

"Yes, go now. You can help unload when you get back." She decided to find out more about the cabin addition and then see if the men could help start unloading the cradles and heavy things. She found that she was relieved that she was home first—not that she thought he'd say anything or rebuke her.

She made only a few changes in the cabin addition. The two rooms and hallway with a separate loft over the addition was a good plan, but she never expected to have it finished before his return. "He didn't come back with you, Dennis?" Dennis had unloaded the feed and put Abe and Sarah in the pasture, before he ventured up to Lorrie's cabin.

Dennis stood on the front porch facing Lorrie and Davy. "Nope, a wagon master at the fort offered him good money to guide his train as far as he could, while the weather was still good. When he found out that Barrett Lee was there, he tracked him down. Barr said that he could use the money for the cabin addition; he paid for the feed too. He said that he didn't expect his wife to support him."

Lorrie was speechless. They'd never discussed money. She was used to paying for what she needed. Again, she'd never thought to ask about what he thought. "Isn't it late to be taking a train through?"

"A few trains have started late. Depends on the weather. He said to tell you to ask me, if you need help."

Lorrie snorted. "I always do. Well, come in and see how the addition looks." The first thing he noticed as he went into the cabin was the cradle sitting at the foot of the bed. She saw him look at it, and said, "I brought another one back besides mine; it's at the general store."

Lorrie counted two and a half snows before they returned. Gray Cloud was shaking the snow off from the half storm, when she heard Jake galloping up from the barn and met her husband and the wolf on the front porch. "You're back in time," she told him.

"So I see." He reached toward her bulging stomach and hesitated. She took his hand and put it on her stomach and then moved closer and leaned against him. "Did you know when I left?"

"Yes, but I didn't see the need to worry you about it." She decided not to tell him yet about her trip while he was gone. That'd wait until he saw the cradle at least.

"Where's Davy?" The snow was getting thicker so they moved inside. "He's not out in this, is he?"

"'Course not. He's finishing up the chores in the barn. He'll be in for supper, soon." Then she smelled the burning potatoes and headed for the stove. Barr took off his coat and hung it near the stove to dry. Looking around the cozy cabin, he spotted the cradle and went over to it.

"Did you get this at the general store? I guess the Johnsons do have everything now."

"Actually, I had to go to Wayside to get it, and I wanted more food for winter too."

"So, you planned that before I left?" He sighed. "Thank you for not worrying me with that either." He remembered Brock's warning and smiled at her. "It's a good thing I had the chance to bring in some money." Then he remembered the addition. "Did you like my plans?" He paused before heading for the door that led there.

Lorrie let him lead the way, and they both admired the two rooms separated from the main room by a hallway. Each room had a small stove for heating, and there were stairs at the end of the hallway going to the loft. Every wall was chinked and tight. There would be room and warmth for a growing family.

Early in July, Lorrie was in the front room lying in the big bed with Barr there to hold her hand whenever she reached for it. Hannah and Lizzie hovered nearby. Davy had been sent to the Johnsons on an errand to keep him away. They couldn't keep Jake from off the porch where he pushed his head in now and then. Cloud stayed off the porch so Jake wouldn't step on him as he leaped on and off the porch. As the time neared, Lorrie noticed the sweat on her husband's face and sent him away, and the two women closed the door and delivered a baby girl.

"Samantha Ann Lee." Lorrie woke up later that night to find Barr looking down at her and their daughter. "Samantha Ann Lee," he whispered again. Lorrie smiled, enjoying the adoring look in his eyes—a look that deepened when he turned his head and looked at her. "I love you," he said, still whispering, so as not to wake the baby, and he bent over and kissed her forehead before going back to his bed of blankets on the floor. He had absolutely refused to join her in their bed until the baby was safe in her cradle.

Lorrie drifted back to sleep after thinking that she would have to tell him that in the morning—to start with. Hard to believe that they'd been too busy to say that as often as they should. Well, obviously not too busy. She was still smiling when her eyes closed.

Sam, sometimes called Sal—learned to walk hanging on to Gray

Cloud's coat. She'd begun crawling on the front lawn around Jake's feet, who never stirred until she was safely away. Her first word was Mother only because Barr was in town that day. When he came home, her next word was Father because Lorrie had been coaching her. "I was sure her first word would be Jake or Cloud," Lorrie said to Carrol, who'd stopped by with fresh made bread and a small slab of butter.

"Cloud can hardly keep up with her anymore," Carrol remarked. Lorrie looked at the old wolf and frowned. Just then Cloud put on a burst of speed to run in a big circle around her before streaking into the woods.

"Barr must be coming," Lorrie said, and went down the steps to take Sam to meet her father. Davy was with Barr and leading their horses when they met.

When Sam was four, Gray Cloud could no longer keep up with her and spent most of his time on a bed on the porch, or up on the hill overlooking the cabin, and in late fall he didn't come down one night. Lorrie, Barr, Sam, Davy, and Jake went up to check on him. Barr had already made a couple trips up to give him water and offer him food.

"He wouldn't touch the venison," Barr told her, before sitting down beside him. Cloud raised his head and put it on Barr's leg and rested it there while Barr stroked his head. The sun was beginning to paint the clouds pink and red when Cloud's head slipped off and rested on the ground.

"Will you get a shovel, Davy, and his new red blanket, please. I didn't want to bring them up here till I had to. I'm going to bury him here." He stopped, choking and swallowing. Sam left her mother's side and crept to the body.

"Cloud," she said and pulled on his coat. "Get up, Cloud." Her mother pulled her away and held her in her lap.

"He can't, honey. Leave him be." Lorrie looked at her husband's form bending over the wolf and cradling his head, and she began weeping, not only for Cloud, but for her husband's loss. Sam looked at Cloud, her father and mother and began sobbing.

Davy looked at them and choked back his grief so that he could say, "I'll bury him for you, Barr."

Barr shook his head violently. "No, I have to do it."

"Maybe you can spell him later, Davy. Just wait for now." She held the blanket, and Sam took hold of it too, holding it to her face and rocking back and forth. But Barr dug the grave by himself. It gave him something to do, Lorrie realized, and he didn't have to look at the body until he thought it deep enough.

After he carefully wrapped Cloud in his blanket, he jumped into the grave and Davy handed the body down. They took turns filling in the grave and packing the dirt down. Lorrie stood on one side of Barr and Davy on the other, and she held Sam close. Jake sniffed the fresh dirt and took up his place behind Lorrie. She waited to give Barr the chance to say good-bye.

"Lord, you know that Gray Cloud was the best wolf, the best dog, the best friend a man could ever have. Take care of him 'til I come and tell him he won't be forgotten, and I hope he's waiting when I get there and not off chasing a deer some place. 'Course we know he ain't gonna catch one of your deer up there, but he's sure going to have fun trying. Thank you, Lord, for letting him stay with me this long. Amen."

Lorrie knelt down beside the grave crying, but managed to choke out an Amen, so Sam added her Amen and so did Davy, who'd given up trying not to cry, though Lorrie thought maybe he was finally crying for his loss, too.

Lorrie wanted to stay until Barr came down the hill, but maybe he'd rather be alone. While she wavered, he touched her shoulder and nudged her forward, and then he picked up Sam. "If you bring the shovel, Davy, I'd be obliged," he said. When they left, Jake was still standing by the grave.

"You don't think he'll try to dig him up, do you?" she worried.

"No. He knows he's dead." The mule was in the front yard the next morning, but he could be found grazing on the hill now and then, near the grave as gold and yellow leaves drifted down and blanketed it.

Lorrie waited for a couple weeks to tell Barr that she was pregnant again, but one night he ran his hand over her stomach and then leaned over her. "When were you going to tell me this time?" he asked.

"No need to spring it on you," she told him.

"I'm fine. No need to coddle me," he informed her. She merely sat up beside him and hugged him tight, until he sighed and laid his head on her shoulder. "You know I miss him, but that doesn't mean I can't go on living and loving."

"I can feel his love still here," she said, but didn't let herself cry because she would never feel the loss he did, nor belittle it with her tears.

Lorrie's second child, another girl, was born in June, and so they named her Penelope June. And not long after that, Davy came back from a trip to Lotawater, and waited until Lorrie was alone on the porch churning butter to give her his news. "You know I'm keeping my eye open for pups and kittens, and I got word of a litter on a farm practically in the woods so I rode down to see it. It was a litter that looked like it had a lot of Gray Wolf's blood in it. One puppy looked a lot like he might have looked when he was a puppy, but I had to ask if you thought that Barr would like one."

Lorrie sat still, thinking. "I don't think so. It's hard on an animal to live up to an owner's expectations, but I certainly want to see them. Let's go there tomorrow. I'll tell Barr that I have to get supplies. After all, I'm always thinking of something little Penny needs. Are any of them spoken for? Should we go now?"

"No, not many folks want a wolf dog because of their livestock, but I don't think the farmer'll put them down. I told him I was interested, and knew some others who might be interested."

Lorrie would have liked to have had Barr go with her, but she never wanted to do anything that would hurt him either, so early the next morning she and Davy headed out. She rode Shadow, with Jake running alongside. The farmer took them out to the barn where five puppies wrestled in the straw while their mother, a collie, watched. No wonder they looked so much like what would have had to be their grandfather or great grandfather, and then she saw the white puppy. It would have been hard to ignore the puppy chewing on her leather riding skirt.

She sat down and gathered the little female in her lap. "Blizzard. I'll call you, Blizzard," she crooned to the puppy. Davy and the farmer exchanged glances. This one had found a new home.

Then she saw the one that resembled Gray Cloud. She turned it over on its back and sighed. "He looks too much like Cloud. It wouldn't be fair to either of them." She turned to the farmer, "Do any of these others have a home yet?"

"My daughter wants the other gray, the female that's not so dark, and I plan to take the rest to sell so they're not around here and no one can blame me if they bother livestock."

"Good idea," Lorrie said. "I'll train this one not to do that."

"Good luck with that," he said with a slight grin. "She tried to tackle a hen the other day. The rooster came down on her right sharp, so she probably won't bother chickens again."

"Good start," Lorrie said gratefully. "I'm glad to hear it. They're weaned, aren't they?" The puppy's sharp teeth made that probable.

"Yep. Ready to go. I'm asking a dollar for that one," he added.

Good price, Lorrie thought, though she knew someone whose dog was named Fourbucks because that was what the mother paid for him, and her family nicknamed the dog that, and it became a family joke.

As she carried the pup outside, Jake trotted up to sniff her, and she licked his nose, and he snuffled in her coat. "Looks like they'll get along fine," the farmer said. "I saw the mule wandering around, but I figured there was a reason you let him loose."

"He thinks he's a dog," she said automatically, and "I think he'll enjoy having another one around." On the way home, she wondered what Barr would think. "She doesn't look too much like Gray Cloud, does she?" She looked to Davy for reassurance.

"We can shave her coat off," he said.

Lorrie was in the cabin, trying to coax a stubborn puppy to drop her moccasin, when Barr came in. Before she knew he was there, he had passed her and picked the puppy up. "Drop it," he said sharply. The surprised puppy dropped the moccasin and tried to escape, but Barr held her firmly. "Yours?" he asked.

"Yes, I saw her down the trail and couldn't come all the way back to get your permission."

He looked at her and frowned. "I would think not. This is your home; but have you introduced her to Penny yet?"

"No, I was waiting for you so there'd be two of us to watch."

"Oh, yes. Might as well get started. Put Penny on the floor."

Lorrie spread a blanket on the floor and sat down by the baby. Barr squatted on the other side and put the puppy down just off the blanket. Blizzard eyed the baby and watched the man for a minute before deciding to investigate. She crept up on the baby who was kicking her feet in the air and cooing and then grabbed the ribbons dangling off her booties. "Drop it," Barr snapped.

The dog hesitated, then tugged again and found herself in the air and the ribbons removed from her mouth. Barr put her down next to the little feet and waited. Blizzard moved one paw forward and found herself on her back. She yipped and tried to scramble away. Barr held her firmly until she stopped struggling. When he released her she scuttled under Lorrie's skirt and peeked out.

"We'll have to watch her, but she's responsive, and she didn't try to bite me."

"I thought I'd put a long line on her and tie her to Jake when she's outside and tie her to the table leg when we're inside."

"And she'll sleep in Davy's room 'til we can trust her." Lorrie didn't like that, but it was only wisdom. She hoped Blizzard wouldn't think she was Davy's dog. But it was Lorrie who fed her and played with her, and she ended up sleeping in Sam's room until she was older. And one day when Lorrie was sitting outside with Penny while she shucked corn, it was Blizzard who killed the snake she found crawling on the baby's blanket.

"It was only a corn snake, and she probably would have killed it anyway," Lorrie admitted, "but she got between the snake and Penny."

"We'll keep watch, but she seems trustworthy. Jake doesn't seem to be watching her as much. Of course, Peaches kicking her into the fence when she tried to nip her heels helped teach her respect for the cows."

Lorrie nodded. Barr had checked her out for damage later after she finally left Lorrie's side; her leg was bruised, but she soon stopped limping and watched all the cows suspiciously.

Chapter Seventeen
~ A New Chapter ~

Lorrie was on the porch working her way through a pile of clothes that needed to be mended, looking up now and then to be sure that Sam and Penny were still romping with Blizzard as Jake grazed on the grass at the edge of the woods. Blizzard barked once, but Jake was already moving into the woods to circle what must be strangers coming up the road from the valley.

As two riders approached, she recognized the pinto and the buckskin as horses from Journey's Rest, the Carruthers' hotel. A young man was on the frisky pinto, and his companion was riding the placid buckskin. They bore a striking resemblance to each other, possibly even twins, she speculated as they reined their horses in at the porch steps.

The boy shifted in his saddle uneasily and flushed, as the girl asked, "Are you Lorrie Lee?"

Lorrie put the basket of mending aside and stood up. "Yes," she acknowledged. "Can I help you? And please light and come up on the porch. Sam, get some water for our guests."

The girl was off her horse in a flash and fumbling in her saddlebag, and she pulled out a book, waving it in triumph. "I knew I could find you!" she said, glancing at the boy. "I'm Clara Thompkins, and this is my brother, Carl. He didn't want to come, but Mom and Dad wouldn't let me look for you by myself. And none of them thought I could find you because it was just a book and it couldn't possibly be true."

Lorrie laughed at her enthusiasm. "May I see it, please?" Sam and Penny crowded in close to look too. Yes, it was Nancy Chandler's book,

A Woman's Way West. Lorrie had the copies Nancy had sent her, but it was interesting seeing a well-worn and cherished copy that belonged to a reader. She sat down on the porch steps to look at the pictures. This was an early edition and didn't have all the photos that Nancy had added to a later edition.

Carl had finally dismounted and tied both horses to the hitching rack; now he was casually looking around. "Is this Jake?" he asked as the mule shoved his way through the two horses to sniff the stranger. So, despite his purported disbelief, he'd read the book—or at least looked at the pictures.

After Clara had gotten over her awe, she scratched underneath Jake's ears and stroked his neck. Then she looked around, dismissing Blizzard with a glance. "Where's Gray Cloud?" she demanded.

"Good heavens, Clara," her brother said, embarrassed. "Don't you know how old your book is?!"

Lorrie laughed at the siblings. Maybe the next one will be a boy, she suddenly hoped. That would be an interesting addition. She wasn't sure yet that she was pregnant again, and she hadn't mentioned the possibility to anyone, since she planned to visit Victoria and her newest child as soon as Barr got back from his hunting trip with Brock.

"I'm sorry," Clara apologized. "I never thought. He looks so alive."

"It's all right. It's been a while now, and I appreciated your sharing your book with me. If you want, we can walk up the hill to where he's buried. The whole group, consisting of two sisters, a brother and a sister, an old mule, and a young white dog climbed the hill and stood by the grave. There was an engraved rock at the head of it now. Barr had carved Gray Cloud's name; Lorrie had planted flowering shrubs, and Jake kept the grass short.

Clara timidly touched Lorrie's sleeve. "May I pick some of the flowers and put them on his grave?" she asked hopefully. Lorrie saw that she wanted not only to honor him, but to make a connection, so she simply nodded. She handed the girl her boot knife when she had trouble breaking the branches off.

She invited them to lunch. That was something she did now and then, so they wouldn't think she couldn't cook, from reading the book. She looked back, and paused to admire the flowers and remember the wolf as he had been, before turning to go back to the cabin. She almost fell over Blizzard, who appeared to be thinking of grabbing her skirt to nudge her along.

After a lunch of toast, cheese, sausage, and potatoes with leftover apple pie—a gift from Hannah—Lorrie took them all on a tour of her cabin; she pointed up the hill to where other cabins were hidden in the trees, and then they all rode down to the hotel to meet Clara and Carl's parents. Sam and Penny rode double on Shadow, and Lorrie rode Sunny, who still had a scar on her neck from a bullet graze, but her mane covered it so no one asked about it.

"You see," Clara said, "Here she is!"

Mr. Tompkins smiled and shook her hand. "I'm not the fan that my daughter is, but she had me read the book, and I was very impressed." Lorrie thought he might be wondering how much of it was true, but she couldn't say that it was or that it barely scratched the surface, so she said, "I like the way Nancy Chandler gave us all credit for settling Sugar Valley, and it is true that the valley is named after a dog. As for Jake and Gray Cloud, you would have had to see them in their prime."

He nodded seriously. Now he was impressed. He'd wondered how she would talk about the book that made her a heroine of the old west—a west that was disappearing, even though Indians were still a danger here and there—and not always so much there.

"Here's Jake now, Father!" Clara pointed excitedly to the black mule that was beginning to turn to shades of gray. Jake trotted up to the girl to see what she wanted when she called his name.

"Tell him it's all right, Clara. That you were just talking about him and don't need his help. And tell him to take Sunny and Shadow to the hotel corral." Lorrie knew she was showing off, but she wanted to give people a taste of what they could do.

Clara stood still and repeated the words to herself. Then she faced the mule, and said, "Jake, take Sunny and Shadow to the hotel corral," and she pointed at it. Lorrie hid a smile. Clara wanted to help him.

Jake backed up, circled the two horses, untied their reins, laid his ears back, and stamped a front hoof. They were used to being herded by him so they raced to the corral with Jake holding both reins in his mouth, racing along between them.

Mr. Thompkins turned to Lorrie and slowly closed his mouth. "I bet there's a lot that's not in that book."

She nodded. "I couldn't tell her everything for different reasons."

"And the book wouldn't hold it all either, I think."

"It couldn't," she told him, remembering just some of the scenes—and her friends. "But I want to say, sir, that it was a pleasure meeting Clara—and being appreciated." She blushed. "I mean. I am, here, but to be known beyond my little world, is an interesting experience."

The Thompkins had actually come to Sugar Valley only to allow Clara to track down the woman in the book, and the entire family was pleased to find Lorrie and the valley not to be a disappointment. Carl even rode up the last day to say good-bye to Jake, who blew in his ear and rubbed his head against his shoulder, so that Carl did not feel left out on his sister's pilgrimage.

Sam and Penny enjoyed the visit, though they didn't exactly know why the visitors had come. Barr and Brock had returned before the visitors left, but they retreated to the Summers' cabin.

Davy's father returned one day, and Davy spent most of his time with his father, but stopped by on the girls' birthdays and holidays to exchange gifts and see Lorrie and Barr. "He's lonely," he told them, "and I miss you all, and I will remember this as being home."

"It will always be your home, David," Barr told him. Lorrie hugged him. "Always," Lorrie echoed. "And the girls miss their big brother."

Lorrie visited Vicky, Bolt, Marcus, and little Keith before her son was born. "Timothy Jason Lee," she told Elizabeth and Hannah as they wrapped him in a blanket. She had talked to Barr about it after she told him she was pregnant again. "The book and the Thompkins made me think about how history is lost when no records are kept. And, of course, sometimes people don't know if it's true, but the family should know."

Barr agreed. "I know more about you from the book, and it showed me what questions to ask. Those two deserve to be remembered."

Lorrie nodded. "We all do," she said. "We forget when we get busy; and we think we'll always be here to tell the newcomers."

She still recalled the embarrassment of stopping for an anticipated meal at the home of a woman she'd helped in Rocky Falls. She'd met her when the woman had come to her on one of her supply trips to sell whatever Lorrie wanted to buy. She and her daughter had been left while her husband and son went to the gold fields. The women ran out of money and supplies, and were desperate and starving when they got word of Lorrie looking to fill her wagon on one of her early trips. Lorrie didn't need any of the furniture she was offered, but she gave them money in trade for future meals.

She was still flushed and annoyed when she recounted her experience to Carrol. "They were German immigrants, and I was so looking forward to one of her meals of sauerbraten and potato dumplings. I hadn't even had lunch that day because I was so close to her home, and I had sent her word, as I always did, by the boy at the livery stable, where I'd stabled Shadow that morning, while I visited Ink at his newspaper."

She paused and shook her head. "Well, her husband and boy were back and at the table when I knocked. The wife invited me in, but seemed nervous. I'd sat down at a place set for me, when the husband started in, asking me why I was there. He demanded to know why I was taking advantage of his wife, her hospitality, her food. He was red in the face and shouting, and the boy kept nodding in agreement with him. Mother and daughter never said a word. I was so very hungry, and the meal was delicious as always, but that sort of thing does take the edge off your appetite, and the two women looked so appalled and scared that I finally gave up. I stood up with all the dignity I could muster, and thanked him for his hospitality and courtesy to a stranger. Then I left. I was so angry!"

"None of you explained?"

Lorrie shook her head. "They were obviously too afraid. Maybe he left them money and told them that that would take care of their needs. 'Course, it didn't. He was gone almost three years, I believe. After I got over being angry and feeling vengeful, the thought came to me, that maybe it was a lesson I needed to learn. That not everyone knew me or was beholden to me. And I felt a trifle ashamed. Not much, but a trifle."

Carrol laughed. "You could have sent him a copy of your book with a chapter devoted just to ingrates."

Lorrie laughed and shook her head. "The more I think of it, the more I'm grateful for the lesson, lest I become too arrogant, and feel that I can stop and rest on my laurels."

Little Timmy was crawling onto the porch when Blizzard dragged him back into the house by the seat of his pants. "Thank you, Blizzard," Lorrie said, and she closed the door to the porch, so she didn't see Jake take off to meet another visitor. Feeding Timmy and checking to see if the bread had risen, she was surprised by a knock on the door. She was heading for it when Jake pushed it open. It was a trick he'd mastered long ago unless the bolt was in place.

"Nancy! I wasn't expecting you!"

Nancy Chandler laughed. "The mail is still chancy out here, I see. Where's the family?" then she noticed Timmy in his high chair. "I didn't know you had another one!"

Lorrie shook her head. "I can't blame it on the mail. I've just been busy. Barr and the girls are in town. I think they're buying me birthday presents. I'm not supposed to know, but all those questions about what I really want, were a clue. And Davy is probably going to stop by, too. We always made certain that he got his share of presents."

"Well, here's another birthday present, then. A new edition of my book is coming out. I'm adding more pictures. Some I have that weren't used, and I thought some new ones of the children and anything else you'd like to add would make it even better. She brought out one of her notebooks and laid it on the table. The photographer is at the hotel. I can have him come up here or we can go down there. Whatever you wish."

"Both," Lorrie said decisively. "I want more pictures of the others and their children, especially the ones who've grown up, now—and the wives and husbands. It's hard keeping track of them all. I'll send word to Carrol and her husband, Dennis and his wife, and Star and her father and mother. I definitely want her and Davy and the Browns in this edition so everyone can see what makes a community."

"I'll start a list right now so we don't leave anyone out," Nancy said. "The editor wants this edition even bigger, because it's selling so well. What? Where's my notebook?"

Lorrie looked around. Timmy was still in his high chair, but Blizzard was sneaking outside with the notebook in her mouth. "Blizzard, you bring that back right now! Go get her, Jake! Save the notebook!" Nancy sat down on the porch steps and couldn't stop laughing.

The End.

About the Author

Joy V. Smith has been writing since she was a little kid and made her own little books--complete with covers. She loved to read, and she wanted to create books too. She lives in Florida--inland safe from hurricanes, except for 2004 when Charley, Frances, and Jeanne came through and wreaked havoc. Downed trees and blue tarps everywhere.

While her favorite genre is science fiction, she writes fantasy, romance, and children's stories--and non-fiction so she's used to research. She's written mostly short stories, which have been published in print magazines, webzines, anthologies, and two audiobooks, including *Sugar Time*. *Detour Trail* is her first western, and she spent a lot of time with maps and books.

Contact the author at:

My writing blog: http://pagadan.wordpress.com/
My media blog: http://pagadan.livejournal.com
My house blog: http://pagadan.blogspot.com/